'*The Key to Finding Jack* is ful
A brilliant read and

Alison Brumwell, Chair of CILIP Youth
Libraries Group

'Celebrating the importance of community,
family and friends, [*The Cooking Club Detectives*]
is a lovely, warm-hearted story that shows how
food can bring people together.'

The Week Junior, Book of the Week

'Superb. A book for those of us who are on the side
of dragons. Which really means everyone.'

Sue Chambers, Waterstones Finchley Road on
The Dragon in the Bookshop

'I love Ewa's books... with their colourful, charismatic
characters and pacy plots they always engage
and entertain.'

Richard Simpson, KS2 teacher and children's
book reviewer

'*The Wolf Twins* is a beautifully written and deeply
empathic story that celebrates the unique bond between
twins and the healing and transformative powers of nature.
Reminding us we are all made of stardust this book is an
absolute triumph that will soothe your soul and
completely capture your heart.'

Kevin Cobane, teacher and children's
book reviewer

THE WOLF TWINS

EWA JOZEFKOWICZ grew up in Ealing and studied English Literature at UCL. Her debut novel, *The Mystery of the Colour Thief*, was shortlisted for the Waterstones Children's Book Prize, 2018. Her novels, *Girl 38: Finding a Friend*, *The Key to Finding Jack*, *The Cooking Club Detectives* and *The Dragon in the Bookshop* are also published by Zephyr. Ewa lives in London with her husband and twin daughters.

For Daisy
from
Ewa Jozefkowicz

Also by Ewa Jozefkowicz

THE WOLF TWINS

Ewa Jozefkowicz

ZEPHYR

An imprint of Head of Zeus

A catalogue record for this book is available from the British Library.

ISBN (PBO): 9781801109239
ISBN (E): 9781801109215

Cover design: Katy Riddell
Typeset by Ed Pickford

Printed and bound in Great Britain
by CPI Group (UK) Ltd, Croydon CR0 4YY

Head of Zeus Ltd
First Floor East
5–8 Hardwick Street
London EC1R 4RG
WWW.HEADOFZEUS.COM

To Julia and Magda

1

Watchful Lucy

I see her in the clearing outside our house the day after the snowstorm. Weather-beaten, with matted hair, like a well-worn, bobbly jumper. Her white beard of frozen fur has a smattering of frost, and her beady eyes are wild. She turns her head, as if searching for something. My hand hesitates at the window latch. Right now, this single pane of glass is the only thing separating our worlds.

I've never seen a wolf this close before. I stare at her, and she looks back questioningly. Time hangs between us. I'm trying so hard not to blink that my eyes sting.

'Who are you?' I whisper, because even without asking Mum I sense she's not one of hers.

The she-wolf opens her jaws and lets loose a growl. I tense, though I know it's not a sound of anger, but perhaps of hunger, or pain.

She startles, and I watch as her back arches and she flees into the forest so fast it's as though she was never here at all.

Then our front door creaks and I hear pounding feet, and before she comes into my line of vision, I know it's Alpha. She hasn't noticed the wolf that she's scared off. She flings her bag over her shoulder and jogs down the path, slipping slightly in the snow.

I watch her feet rise from the ground in their dirty trainers (she wouldn't be seen dead in clean ones) and come crashing down, droplets of slushy snow spraying our front step. Her feet are constantly in motion, as if she's always dribbling on the basketball court, gearing up for a super slam dunk. Alpha is so confident, I'm certain she can do anything. She's technically my mirror image. We have the same wavy ginger hair (except hers is always smoothed back into a messy bun, so it doesn't get in her way), the same round face with a smattering of freckles across the nose and cheeks, and the same long, thin legs. But inside we couldn't be more different.

I try to imagine what it must feel like, not being scared of what people think or what they might say. Even leaving the house on my own seems impossible. If I close my eyes, I can just about see it – waltzing up the steps of the bus or along the street to school... or maybe... No, I wouldn't waste it on school.

If I could walk out of the house without a care in the world, I would go somewhere extra special. I'd hop on the train to London and visit the observatory in Greenwich. I'd find the right bus by myself and use the map on my phone to navigate the way up the hill. Then I'd gaze down at the park, the Queen's House, the winding river, and the city in the distance, and I'd stay until it got dark. And then Alpha and I — because she'd be there with me — we'd go and look through the 28-inch refractor telescope and see the moon. And we'd think about how it must have felt to be the first human to walk on its surface...

2

Racing Alpha

I run from Gra's house to the bus stop, like a jungle explorer running from a leopard or a tiger. I'm probably not far off. Who knows what animals lurk here? All these tall trees give me the creeps, like the stupid rickety bus that comes only once an hour and looks about a hundred years old.

Who would want to live in a place like this?

When I told Hector we were moving to the forest, he thought I was having him on.

'What, like Tarzan? Maybe you could try out a fresh move – swinging from a vine in the treetops to drop the ball in the net?'

His eyes creased up and he laughed so hard his glasses almost fell off. That sparked another wave of rage inside me about the ridiculous unfairness of it all.

'I wish I was joking,' I told him. 'But Mum's got a new job and we're going next month. Apparently there's no discussion.'

'What? But you've always lived next door to us, Allie,' he wailed. 'She can't just decide you're leaving without asking you.'

'Of course she can. My parents are great at making selfish decisions. First Dad, now her.'

I'd stopped speaking to Dad when he moved out and it became clear we weren't good enough for him any more. Now I felt like walking out on Mum, but it's tricky as she's the parent we agreed to live with.

'What am I going to do without you?' Hector asked miserably.

'Probably get into less trouble,' I said, hoping that would make him laugh, but it didn't.

He kicked the garden wall we were sitting on with the back of his foot. A fleck of white paint floated to the ground like a giant snowflake.

'Where is this forest? And what is your mum going to do?'

'She's going to be… wait for it – a rewilder.'

'A what?'

'I know – I can't believe it's even a job. Sometimes I think she's made it up. She'll be helping to bring back wolves into Whitecastle Forest.'

'What… like *real* wolves?'

I nodded grimly.

'But isn't that super dangerous? Why is that a good idea?'

'You'd have to ask her.'

I climbed down the ladder that straddled our gardens. Luce and I would climb it to play with Hector, pretty much since we could walk. By the end of February, it would have to be removed, along with the collection of special stones we'd gathered on our adventures and which we'd proudly displayed along the wall.

'What about school, Allie?' Hector asked, panicking.

'I'll be there. Don't you worry,' I said firmly. Mum was trying to make us both move to Whitecastle

School, especially after Luce's Incident, but that's something I wouldn't budge on. Jefferson Secondary is where Hector and Vern and all my other friends are – not to mention Mr Ray, the best basketball coach ever. This year we're in with a decent chance of winning the inter-school mixed basketball championships.

Mum had protested that it was almost a forty-minute journey on the bus each way, but I said I'd do it.

So here I am, on the bus with 'the usuals'. There's the woman in the colourful shirts and pristine suits, sitting at the back with her laptop open. She clearly works in town, but I have no idea why she chose to live out here. There's the old man with his equally old black Labrador, who always travel on Tuesdays and Fridays, and there are the two boys in red uniform. They look like brothers. One of them is always reading and the other looks like he's playing games on his phone. I've said hi to them a couple of times, but they didn't seem keen on talking.

The roads are slippery because of the ice and snow – mad weather for the start of April. The bus trundles along slowly out of the forest. It hasn't been repaired in years, and the potholes make us bounce in our seats, which I can tell is particularly annoying for the colourful-shirt-laptop-lady who's trying to type.

It's only when we reach the turn onto the main road that takes us into town that I finally breathe a sigh of relief, because I feel as though I'm coming home.

3

Anxious Lucy

'Breakfast is served, m'lady. Scramblies today, if you please.'

Gra's face appears round the side of my door.

He catches me, still kneeling by the window. I'm half hoping the wolf might come back, but it hasn't.

Gra isn't like most grandfathers. He has long grey hair, which he wears in a thin ponytail, and he's tall and strong. He looks like he should be the leader of a powerful tribe. Gra has knowledge that runs deep, but he only offers it when the time is right and he knows you're truly listening. Not just with your ears, but with your heart.

What I love most about him is that there are no whispers or hushed voices, like other adults. He always tells you exactly what he thinks.

'There was a wolf out there. Really close.'

'Ah,' he says, raising an eyebrow.

'It's not one of Mum's,' I say.

'How could you tell?'

'She's shown us photos, and this one looked different. Her coat seemed to shine in the sun. She wasn't dark brown like the others. She had tiny specks of white. At first I thought it was the snow, but I realised it was the pattern of her fur.'

'Well. Perhaps it's another type of wolf, then,' says Gra calmly, but I get the feeling there's something he isn't telling me. I know to wait until he's ready to talk.

I like the quiet moments in the mornings when it's just Gra and me, after Mum has gone to work and Alpha to school. It's a time when we eat breakfast and I swirl the spoon in my tea as Gra tells me about interesting 'threads' of his life in Whitecastle.

Gra has had more jobs than anyone I know. He's been a builder, a zoologist, a farmer and a chef. I'm sure there are others he hasn't even mentioned.

I open my mouth to ask, when he says: 'Lucy, Mr Pang called.'

My spoon clatters in my cup and splashes some tea. I put it down to stop my hands shaking. I'm suddenly not hungry any more.

'The prospect of going back to school must be nerve-racking,' says Gra gently. 'But your mum thinks it's best. And she could be right. You're twelve, Lucy – what a magnificent age. You should be out there with your friends, enjoying yourself, being silly, discovering the world. You shouldn't be stuck here with an old fuddy-dud like me.'

When he says this, I stifle a laugh. Gra couldn't be less of a fuddy-dud if he tried.

'Your mum has set up a meeting with Mr Pang. She thinks perhaps you could go back after the break.'

I can see from the way Gra is looking at me that he doesn't think it's a good idea. But Mum has asked him to talk to me and he can't refuse his daughter.

'I can't go back,' I say simply.

Gra nods. He doesn't say anything more. We've never talked openly about the Incident, but I know he knows. Or, at least, he knows as much as Mum's told him, which is half the story.

I wish I could find the words to tell Gra exactly what happened. They're stuck deep inside me and the thought of prising them out makes my hands shake even more. I sit on them and look at the table instead.

4

Winning Alpha

The ref's whistle pierces the air and I've never heard a sweeter sound.

'A-llie! A-llie!' Margot slaps me on the back. The blood pumps in my head. I've got a real chance of getting into the Under-15s team, even though I'm not yet thirteen. That would be mega. Then I just need a scout to notice me and I'll be on my way to America as a professional basketball player!

Cheers from the stands drown Mr Ray's closing remarks, but I hear the words 'Player of the Match is Alpha Mickleswick', and I'm so ecstatic I forgive him for using my first name, which is only used by my family. I collapse on the bench beside Hector, who is clapping so hard the palms of his hands must hurt.

'I knew it,' he keeps repeating, though he's shaking his head as though he doesn't actually believe it. Neither do I – not quite.

Then I see Sula strolling over, as if it's the most normal thing in the world for the Under-15s captain (rumoured to have won a scholarship to one of the biggest basketball academies) to come and speak to *me*.

Sitting down on the other side of the bench, she looks me square in the eye. For a few seconds she doesn't speak, and I think maybe I got it wrong. Maybe she wants to offer me advice. Were my footwork or passes off?

'Un-bel-ievable,' she says eventually. 'Come and join us for training on Thursday.'

I grin and nod stupidly. I seem to have lost my voice. My stomach is sloshing with excited happiness. Happy soup!

I don't know it yet, but her words will play in my head over and over, for hours, for days, for months.

'Anyway, I won't keep you. You probably want to hang out with your family. After a game like that, they should be parading you round the court.'

The happy soup turns sour.

She has no idea, but she's ruined it. She's removed the Jenga piece that my joy was teetering on and my victory is toppling down in slow motion.

'Come on,' says Hector, 'Vern's waiting for us by the candyfloss machine. He's saved us a place.'

I feel sick.

I don't know why I did it. No, that's a lie. I know exactly why I did it, but I feel awful. What makes it worse is Mum, Gra and especially Luce would have loved it. Luce would have carefully tracked every single move of the game.

'You go; I'll join you,' I say to Hector, pretending I need a couple of minutes to get my breath back. I sit with my head between my legs. Eyes closed.

An image comes to my mind. Luce and I are six or seven, watching basketball with Dad. We barely missed an NBA game. We called ourselves the Slam Dunk Trio. She and I would sit together on the big wicker armchair with the worn flowery cushions, wedged in close. She used to edge forward and focus so hard, she almost fell off her seat. I would feel her tense next to me, whole minutes before somebody scored. She knew. I've no idea how, but she did.

Tonight she would have analysed my footwork and told me later where I did a particularly strong tackle, where my spin moves were on point, and where my dribbles took that little bit too long. Luce is great at that. She'd make an awesome coach. But she couldn't be here. Not tonight.

'Allie, you were on fire!' someone shouts, and I open my eyes.

Some of the netball girls from Year 9 are high-fiving me. Mr Stevenson waves from across the court and gives me a double thumbs-up.

'You got lucky, Beanpole,' says Vern, coming back with two clouds of pink candyfloss. 'You think getting the ball in the net a couple of times makes you some kind of hero?'

It took me a while to realise Vern was joking when he said stuff like that. When we joined Year 7, I thought he was being mean to everyone, but he has a weird sense of humour, which is something I like about him.

I grab my towel and drape it round my shoulders like a cape and I put my arms out and pretend I'm Superwoman flying from the top of a huge tower. Vern rolls his eyes, but Hector's cracking up and almost chokes on a crisp.

Later, when we're so full of sweets we could be sick, and we've done a celebratory dance with Sula and the team, we pile into Vern's dad's car. I sit in the back between the two of them, thinking about what I'll say to Luce and Gra when I get home. Mum probably won't be in yet, so at least that will be one less person to hide things from.

'Football practice, was it?' asks Mr Selling, looking at us in the rear-view mirror.

'No, Dad, it was the final of the inter-school basketball championships, and we won.'

'We?' asks Mr Selling. He raises an eyebrow. 'I don't see you wearing your kit.'

'By we, I mean the school,' says Vern, trying not to look deflated. He wasn't selected for the first team for this game, although he's not a bad player.

'Allie totally nailed it! She was a dynamo on the court. She got Player of the Match and everything,' says Hector.

'Wow! That's impressive, Allie. Well done. Your parents will be proud. You've got your eyes on the prize?'

'On the NBA,' I say, then laugh nervously. I can't believe I've said that aloud. But if I can't tell Luce, or Mum or Gra and especially not Dad, Mr Selling will have to do.

'You really need to put your back into it, Vern,' he says, trying and failing to catch Vern's eye in the rear-view mirror. 'If you want to succeed, you need to take note of what others around you have achieved. Set your bar higher.'

'Don't worry, Dad,' Vern answers breezily, although I can see he's boiling up inside. 'I'm headed for Bayville Academy.'

A look passes over Mr Selling's face, as if he doesn't quite believe him. 'Effort is everything, Vern. You'd do well to remember that.'

He might have a point, because Vern does cut corners sometimes – like when he copies Hector's homework – but he doesn't deserve to be told off in front of his friends.

I put my hand on his, squeezing it to reassure him, but he snatches it away as if he's been burned.

'Anyhow, how's your sister doing these days, Allie?' Mr Selling asks, changing the subject.

My heart crashes against my chest. I wish he'd asked any other question.

'She's fine,' I mumble.

'Is she feeling better?'

'Yes,' I say. 'Definitely. There's been progress.' The words tumble out of my mouth, but even as I say them, I know they couldn't be further from the truth. Next to me, Vern readjusts himself in his seat.

'She'll be coming back to school soon?'

'Yeah.' I say. 'I hope so.'

5

Woodland Lucy

When Alpha and I were little, shortly after Nanna died, Gra would invite us over for weekends. In winter, we'd go sledging in the hills on planks of wood we'd found in the shed. When spring came, we'd help him plant carrots, tomatoes and beans, and in summer, we'd go wild swimming.

Later, when Mum got busier and busier at work, Gra would come and stay with us instead, so we didn't get a chance to visit his house in the forest. Until a few months ago, that is, when Mum's friend got in touch about a new job. It was for a much more senior position and was four days a week, meaning she would be able to spend more time with us – a perfect opportunity. Plus, I sensed she wanted to be further from Dad after what Alpha and I called 'the shouting months'.

'What's the job?' I asked, as she told us her news over dinner.

'I'll be leading the wolf rewilding programme at Whitecastle Forest,' she said in a single breath, and we both laughed.

'No, seriously,' Alpha said. 'Is it another job at the university?'

Then she got the contract out of her bag and showed it to us. 'Layham Grey Wolf Rewilding Reserve' it said at the top of the page, and below that: 'Job Title: Chief Rewilding Officer'.

'What do you think? I want to do it. It'll be an adventure.'

Alpha's eyebrows disappeared under her fringe. 'You've never worked with wolves,' she blurted out. 'You've always just researched dogs.'

Mum looked offended. 'It's not just researching dogs, Alpha. It's research into the behaviour of canines, which include foxes, jackals and wolves. And yes, I've mainly been lecturing these last few years, but I'm ready to go back out into the field. I did a three-year placement at the Wolf Conservation Trust before you were born.'

'Why would you want to rewild them? Aren't they dangerous?' asked Alpha. 'They attack humans, don't they?'

'Actually, attacks on humans are very rare. Real life isn't quite the same as *Little Red Riding Hood*. Wolves tend to be scared of us. As for why they're useful – there are many reasons. The main one being biodiversity. Wolves can prevent overgrazing and they help many other species to flourish, mainly through the food opportunities they provide.'

I could tell Alpha wasn't convinced. 'And won't you have to travel for hours to get there?' she asked, confused. 'Where is this rewilding reserve?'

My stomach sank at the thought that Mum was getting a job like Dad, which took him to different places around the world for months at a time.

'Well,' she said, 'that's the other brilliant thing about it. It's a ten-minute drive from Gra's house in Whitecastle.'

'But that's miles away!'

'It's not that far. I could commute, but I thought it would be good for us to have a fresh start. Away from this place,' she said, looking around at the only home Alpha and I had ever known. I stared at the floor where there were faint marks to the left of the table. If I shut my eyes, I could still make out the plasticine city we'd built at Christmas in that exact spot by the patio doors to the garden.

'We could move in with Gra for a while and find a place of our own nearby.'

'Gra's house? That's, like, in the forest...' said Alpha slowly. 'And what about getting to school?'

'Yes, it's in the forest. That's what's beautiful about it. It's surrounded by nature. I thought you could switch to Whitecastle School. It's where I went when I was growing up.'

I glanced up at Alpha's face. She was giving Mum her look of thunder, which I'd only seen her give one other person before – Dad.

'There is no way I'm changing schools,' she said, in a tone that implied it would be dangerous for anyone to question her.

Mum coughed awkwardly, realising her announcement hadn't quite had the effect she'd hoped. But I felt a light, unexpected relief surging through me. Things at school were not good. Little did I know they were about to get a lot worse, and that Gra and Whitecastle would become my lifelines.

Gra's house is old, with airy rooms that sigh with the sound of wood. He designed it himself and even helped build it, after he and Nanna got married. The huge front porch has a swing seat with their initials carved into it, which creaks comfortingly when you sit on it.

The ground floor is a huge open space with furniture arranged around the fireplace. There's a kitchen area along the far wall. A spiral staircase with faded green carpet, worn by years of stomping feet, leads up to Gra's, Mum's and Alpha's bedrooms. I didn't mind sharing with Alpha – we've always shared – but Gra said he had just the place for me and led me up the narrow staircase to the attic. The stairs are new – the wood is still pale and fresh. This is a recent project of Gra's which he completed singlehandedly. He'd converted the dusty attic into a stargazer's heaven.

The window looks out on an other-worldly view. Sometimes, when the dappled sunlight wakes me, filtering through the branches of ancient oaks and snow-covered pines, I imagine I'm a medieval explorer, embarking on a journey through uncharted land.

'Some of the trees in this forest are five times as old as me,' said Gra. 'And when you go out and get lost among them, time stands still.'

The weekend after we'd moved, while Alpha was silently fuming, Gra took us to see a mammoth oak tree called the Emperor of the South. The three of us linked hands around its trunk, but there was enough space for another person.

I breathed in deeply when I touched the bark and in those few moments, I was completely at peace.

'This young man recently celebrated his 420th birthday,' Gra announced. 'He lived through the Renaissance and the Napoleonic Wars, and more recently, the two world wars. How many people have rested under his branches? He's seen more animals and insects than any of us will know.'

Today, Gra and I spent the morning learning about the Industrial Revolution, and the afternoon doing maths – specifically distance–time graphs. As I look at the curve, trying to figure out the answers to the questions Gra has set me, I think back to the Emperor of the South. He's proof that you don't need to travel any distance at all to witness incredible things. A comforting thought, broken by the sound of the doorbell.

It's Alpha. I'm beginning to think she deliberately forgets her key, in protest. As if she's saying this isn't her permanent home and she's just a guest, passing through.

As I open the door, she raises her hand for a high five, and I deliberately miss, which has been our joke since we were about three.

I know Alpha better than anyone in the world, and today I sense there's something different about her. It's as if there are two opposing forces – her entire body seems to move to an excited beat, but in

6

Inconsiderate Alpha

There was a time when Luce and I could read each other's thoughts. Once, when we were six, I had laryngitis and couldn't speak. But Luce brought me exactly what I needed. She'd make hot cranberry tea with a slice of orange and lemon, and sandwiches just how I liked them, with cheese, pickles and splodges of ketchup (even though she hates pickles herself). She'd plump my cushions the moment I felt cramp in my back and change to another TV show as I was getting bored.

I remember wondering whether other people had this superpower too. It soon became obvious they didn't.

'We're the Wonder Twins. We can take over the world,' I told her. We made masks out of cardboard from Dad's thesis folders, with the initials WT in purple felt-tip pen.

A part of me is certain Luce knows what I've done, although she hasn't shown any sign. I should tell her. She would definitely forgive me. But I can't bear to see the look on her face when she hears.

Mum saves me from talking about school because she's stressing about the new cub at her reserve.

'He arrived on Tuesday, and it's now Friday and he's hardly eaten anything. I guess we should be grateful he's drinking water. If things don't improve by tomorrow, I'm going to call the vet.'

'Chill, Mum. He's probably like Luce. Maybe he's feeling nervous; he'll warm up eventually.'

The instant the words are out, I want to swallow them back in. Gra and Mum shoot each other a panicked look.

It's not what I mean. It's not what I mean at all. I want to explain, but Luce is already on her feet and running upstairs. I try to go after her, but Gra puts his hand on my shoulder.

I struggle out of his grasp. 'Let go.'

'Give her a few minutes, Alpha,' he says quietly. 'She lets you know when she's ready to speak.'

I swing round and push him away, harder than I intended, but I don't care because the fury has expanded in my stomach like a balloon, and I'm about to reach bursting point. My ears are ringing like glass ready to shatter.

'You don't know anything!' I hear myself spit. 'You don't know Luce. You think you do because you teach her every day. But sitting in the house is making her worse, not better! She would have been back at school by now if it wasn't for you!'

Gra's eyes widen. He doesn't say anything as I storm out of the house. I try to sit on one of the chopped logs at the bottom of the garden, but it's covered in snow. I'm freezing. The bird noises are so loud they're crowding my brain, and in the end I give up and go back inside to my room. I try to do some geography homework but find myself writing the same paragraph three times.

I can't stand it any longer. I go up the stairs and knock on Luce's door.

She doesn't answer, so I knock louder and walk in. She's in her pyjamas under the duvet, her head propped on a pillow, her big headphones over her ears. Her laptop is balanced on her knees and I can't make out what she's watching. The screen is filled with strange lights and shapes. It looks like footage filmed on a shaky camera.

Abruptly, a man's face comes into focus. He's wearing an orange boiler suit and he's forced into his seat. He's smiling though, and it isn't until he puts on his helmet I realise he's an astronaut.

I sit on the edge of Luce's bed, fascinated. She's seen me, but doesn't say anything. I can tell by the look on her face she's not upset any more. Gra had been right all along.

I watch as the camera pans out and there are men in military uniform giving some kind of salute. Then there's a thick plume of smoke, and the rocket shoots into space. Luce gives a sigh of satisfaction and shuts the laptop.

'What was that?'

'Yuri Gagarin's take-off.'

'Who?'

'The first man in space. Don't you remember when Dad showed it to us?'

'No,' I say honestly.

The mention of Dad always makes the air thicken around me. He still calls every night on the dot of nine to say goodnight. He leaves voicemails which I don't listen to. So far, I've had 137 missed calls – long distance, because he's currently working on a project in Norway. I know he thinks I'll cave soon and answer, but he's wrong. Incorrect. Deluded. He calls Luce too, and she speaks to him. He's taking advantage, because everyone knows she's too kind. He doesn't deserve to be forgiven. He's a deserter.

'Dad told me Gagarin was a farmer's son,' Luce continues. 'Nobody could have expected he'd be the first man to see our planet from space. Just imagine. I don't think there are words to describe what it must have felt like.'

I can't hold it back any longer. 'Luce, I'm sorry for what I said at dinner. I didn't mean it,' I gabble, and feel an instant surge of relief.

'It's OK. I know you didn't.'

'How are you doing?'

'Fine.'

We sit in silence. There's something enormous hiding behind that word, and although I'm Luce's Wonder Twin, I don't understand it.

'Are you going to the meeting with Mr Pang?' I ask.

'No. I can't go back.'

I search desperately for the right words. There's so much I want to say about what happened that day at school. But the words sit there, tripping on the tip of my tongue.

In the end, I nod stupidly. On my way out, Luce takes off her headphones, moving a few strands of hair. I glimpse a bald patch in the light from her bedside lamp. I watch her fingers move to her hair and pull.

7

Restless Lucy

The shakes started just after Mum and Dad had their last and biggest argument. It was as though a motor had started inside me, stirring waves that reached every bit of my body and making me feel sick. My hands moved constantly, unless I was occupied with something.

I accidentally found that playing with my hair helped, and then, when I heard Mum slam the door and say she 'needed to take a walk', I pulled. The long strand came out of my head and I examined it. It was thick, ginger, and curled slightly towards the tip, just like Alpha's. It had caused a short, sharp pinprick to my scalp. For a moment, my hands were still and my body was absorbed by that miniscule twinge of pain.

I tried not to do it at school, because I was sure people would notice. Mikki, who sat with me, had hawk eyes that spotted everything. Here the shaking was worse. It wasn't just in my body, but in my head, so my eyes couldn't focus. In English, words danced on the page, and it was only when I reread them four or five times they began to make sense. In maths, I stared blankly at equations, because nothing Mr Stevens said made any sense.

Teachers started looking at me with furrowed brows. I'd always done pretty well in school. Now I could barely write a sentence. The only lesson in which things were different was physics, where we were studying astronomy. We were taught by Ms Veelam, who is quiet and gentle and knows loads about space. Clearly a lot, lot more than she's supposed to be teaching us – which is the basic stuff about our solar system, the planets and how they orbit the sun. I think she could tell from my homework that space is my passion, and she invited me to join her Astronomy Club which meets every Thursday lunchtime. I asked Mikki whether she wanted to come with me, and she did, but I knew she wasn't that interested.

Most of the kids in Astronomy Club were Year 8s, 9s and 10s. I didn't know any of them, but it didn't matter. Ms Veelam got us doing amazing things, like using geoboards to map constellations. I created the constellation of Centaurus, which was my favourite because I could clearly see the centaur with its long neck and wonky arms. We relived the Apollo space mission in real time through an interactive video that Ms Veelam found online. The club drew me into a new universe. For those forty minutes, every week, I lost myself in the endless details of space.

Then everything changed. With all the shouting and the slammed doors and the awkward dinners, and trying to control my trembling hands, I didn't notice that Ms Veelam's dresses were becoming looser and looser and that beneath them she was growing a baby. Until the day she announced it would be her last club for a while, because she was going to give birth soon. She said we didn't need to worry, because she was being replaced by Mr Bray. I didn't know it yet, but my world was about to change.

This morning, I'm reminded of Ms Veelam, because beside my bed is the old geoboard that

Gra found yesterday. It's basically a wooden square with nails coming out of it. A piece of green wool has been wrapped around some of the nails to make the shape of a slightly wonky creature with a thin snout and a bushy tail.

'A dog or a wolf?' I asked him.

'I think it's a dog. But you'll have to ask your mum. This used to belong to her. I found it in a pantry cupboard.'

'It *is* a dog,' Mum agreed later. 'But it looks like the new cub.'

And I realise with a start how badly I want to meet him.

8
Angry Alpha

'I need to go to the reserve today,' says Mum. We're sitting at the table for Saturday morning breakfast, which is eggs on toast with an avocado and tomato salad. Gra has made the bread himself and the smell fills the kitchen.

I apologised to him for what I'd said, and he ruffled my hair to show we were OK, but for some reason it didn't make me feel any less guilty.

'On your day off?'

'I don't want to leave Tara on her own with the cub,' Mum says. 'She's only been with us three months. She doesn't know how to handle special cases like this.'

'She's on her own today with thirteen wolves?' asks Gra, raising a piece of toast to his mouth.

'What? No, no. Larry and Shiv will be there from 10am. But we have the roofer coming to patch up the hole left after the leak. There's a lot going on and nobody will pay enough attention to the cub.'

'What's his or her name?' asks Luce. Her hair is arranged in a bun at the base of her head.

I can tell she's avoiding my gaze. I wonder if she knows I've seen the bald patch.

'It's a male. He doesn't have one yet. He's just arrived from Italy and he's roughly nine weeks old, but nobody knows for sure. He was found in the Apennine Mountains in Italy with his leg tangled in a bush. There was no sign of his parents or siblings. Apparently the rescue team searched for ages.'

Luce looks so distraught it's as if she's personally reliving the wolf's capture.

'At least he's being well looked after now,' I say.

'He does need a name,' Mum says. 'Lucy, you're good at this kind of thing.'

Luce's cheeks flush red as they usually do when everyone's attention is on her – even if that 'everyone' is us.

'I'm not sure,' she says, slowly. 'I guess I don't know enough about him… You'll have to tell us what he's like. Do you have a photo?'

'Why don't you come with me?' Mum asks, clapping her hands together. 'All of you. You haven't seen the reserve properly – well, apart from you, Dad,' she says, looking at Gra. 'I could use some moral support.'

'I can't. I'm going to Hector's for lunch, remember? It's Josh's birthday.' Josh is four years older and plays basketball for our Under-18s team. He already has a scholarship to the prestigious Bayville Academy, where all the international scouts go to find the next big players. Last week when we were at Hector's, he invited us to his birthday.

'Alpha,' says Mum, nudging me in the ribs to try to make me laugh. 'Come with us. This isn't even your friend's birthday. It's your friend's brother's birthday. You could skip it to hang out with us? We miss you!'

My heart sinks. I can already hear Vern's voice in my ear: 'You gone soft, Mickleswick? Ditching us to be with your mum and Allie 2.0, the inferior model?'

I've lost count of the number of times I've asked him not to call Luce that, but he won't stop.

'But Josh was going to show me how to do the world's best ever bank shot…'

'Surely he'll want to celebrate with his mates and not run a basketball training session on his birthday?' says Mum, and she pulls a comical pleading look, like a wounded puppy, which is supposed to make me laugh, but is actually super annoying.

'I'll come,' Luce says.

'Awesome.'

'It's about time you met these creatures,' Gra says to Luce, smiling, 'I have a feeling you'll get on with them.'

Ah, I see this for what it is – another family photo where I'm out of shot, because it's all about *Lucy, Lucy, Lucy.*

'I might get on with them too,' I say. It comes out as more of a snap. I've suddenly had enough of everything always being about Luce.

'Thank you, Alpha,' says Mum, and she looks over the moon.

42

I message Hector to tell him something important has come up, and half an hour later we're folding ourselves into Mum's battered car and I'm already regretting that I agreed to come. Everything about this place is wrong. The wind roaring in my ears as I leave the house, my feet slipping and sliding on Gra's old decking, my eyes blurring in the snowstorm.

In my mind, my own storm has begun.

9

Charmed Lucy

The forest unfurls around us as we travel south, and it's the most mesmerising scene. The snow that fell yesterday morning hasn't melted because of the freezing temperatures and the world is covered in a crunchy white blanket.

Mum is quiet, concentrating on the road. Alpha somehow persuaded her to let her sit in the front but her words still crackle with anger, and I can tell she doesn't want to be here.

Gra shuts his eyes in the back next to me. I do the same.

'Listen,' he whispers. 'The forest has so many voices.'

To begin with, I can't hear anything except the whirring of the engine. *Grrr - frrp. Grrr - frrrp.*

I dive beneath the noise, exploring what's beyond. Slowly, my ears tune in to subtler sounds. I can distinguish at least four different bird calls. Some are excitable high-pitched shrieks; others melancholy twitters. Somewhere above us, an owl hoots. In the distance, there's a dog barking, and the patter of paws on the ground, and – out of nowhere – a low growl. My eyes fly open. I glance at Gra.

'Did you hear that?' I ask, trying to keep the panic from my voice. 'Is that a bear?'

'A bear? There are no bears round here, love,' says Mum, sounding unfazed.

'So what was it? The growl?'

'I didn't hear anything.'

'You might have heard a wild boar,' says Gra casually. He looks at me with his eyebrows raised, and the corner of his mouth turns up slightly as though he's impressed. There's something he knows that he isn't telling me. Just like Alpha.

The main building of the rewilding reserve is white, and with its coating of snow it's barely visible from the road. We're greeted at the door by a young woman wearing what looks like a ski suit and a deerstalker hat.

'I didn't know you were coming today,' she says, smiling.

'We wanted to check in on the new arrival,' Mum explains. 'These are my daughters, Alpha and Lucy.'

'Allie,' Alpha corrects her, holding out her hand. Her handshake is firm and confident.

'Hi,' I manage. I want to offer my hand too, but I can feel it shaking, so I nod instead.

'Tara.'

Out of the corner of my eye, I see Gra looking around.

'Well, lots has changed here,' he says, amazed.

'Dad used to work here when I was little,' says Mum. 'Only then it was a farm.'

'It's beautiful in summer,' says Gra. 'I always thought it was a bad place for a wolf rewilding reserve, though.'

'What do you mean, bad?' asks Mum.

'Well, the wolves have it good here, don't they? It makes it all the harder to leave. When the snow goes, it will be transformed. On that hill you'll have a sea of wild flowers. The river will start running. There'll be that note of honey sweetness in the air. And you realise how close it is to the Place of Strength?'

'That's true. I wonder if the wolves feel it too,' says Mum. 'I'm sure it doesn't stop them finding new places to run free though.'

'What's the Place of Strength?' I ask.

'It's a magical space among the ancient trees in the forest, and for centuries people have believed it has special healing powers. We'll go there one day. Anyway, do you want to meet the cub now?'

Tara leads us down a narrow corridor to a row of outdoor pens, sheltered from the wind. Mum explains there are two key stages to the rewilding process. The first is to make sure the animals are healthy, eating well and, if they're young, that they're able to fend for themselves. The second is to keep them in a larger, enclosed area, to check they're coping in the semi-wild and to discourage the 'homing instinct' in older wolves. They're clever animals – they can sense where their home is and they'll do everything they can to get there just by moving in that general direction.

I imagine this new wolf must be too small to sense where he came from, somewhere far away in the south.

I feel a swoosh of excitement, then a stab of fear, as I remember this is a wild animal. My hands fly to my hair and I want to pull, pull, pull, but Mum and Gra are looking at me and I can't, so instead I put my hands behind my back.

I have a flashback to when Gra first pointed out a wolf to us. Alpha and I must have been five or six. I thought it was a dog. From a distance it looked like the Alsatian our neighbours used to own. But it wasn't a dog. Its pelt, its strength, its roaming eyes hinted at a kind of freedom. It was a creature of the beautiful, vast wild.

There he is. Less than half the size of that first regal wolf we saw. He tumbles out from behind a wooden hut where I notice some meat has been left on a bone, beside a bowl of kibble.

Mum asks Tara in a voice that prickles with worry, 'Has he touched it?'

'Not really.'

The cub recognises Mum straight away, because

he gets up and begins to walk in our direction. His coat is a warm brown-grey, like the colour of rich-smelling earthy coffee, except for his forehead, where the fur is darker and forms a shape like a cross. When he reaches the edge of the pen closest to us, he doesn't look at Mum. He looks at me.

The inky-black pools of his eyes lock with mine, and I feel a spark of electricity up my neck. I want to put out my hand and feel the softness of his fur, especially the bit between his ears that looks like suede.

He seems to like the tassels at the end of my scarf, because he bats them with his paw and watches them swing, like a puppy would. The scarf is a gift Dad bought for me from the Greenwich Observatory, but I take it off and give it to him. He nuzzles into the wool.

'He seems to like you,' whispers Mum.

'Yeah, he does,' agrees Tara, surprise in her voice. 'He hasn't reacted like this to anyone else. Michael said he was going mad in the night, clawing away at the gate. Look over there.'

'Oh, wow. He was trying to break free,' says Alpha.

I see where they're pointing at. On the inside of the gate, claw marks run down the wood like veins. The lines tear at my heart. He's frightened. He's meant to be wild and ferocious, but in reality he's small and scared.

As I lean closer, he raises his front paws up the plank of wood that separates us and we look at each other through the gap. I reach out and put my hand over his paw before anyone can stop me. I can see the tiny claws, but for the first time in forever, the fear is gone.

'Lucy – don't,' says Mum, but it's too late. The wolf cub and I are connected. We're stronger together.

When I finally let go, he looks at me questioningly. He doesn't drop his gaze. The overhead lights dance in his eyes.

'Claw, look after my scarf for me,' I say out loud and the wolf's eyes widen.

'Claw?' asks Alpha.

'Claw,' Mum repeats. 'I like it. Well, we've found a name. Now our next challenge is to get him to eat.'

'Aren't wolves supposed to hunt?' asks Alpha. 'Maybe he's annoyed you're keeping him here, and he wants to go home and find his own food?' Her right foot is tap, tap, tapping on the floor and I sense there are many other places she'd rather be, the basketball court topping the list.

'Yes,' says Mum. 'But he's too small to hunt for his own food. So he needs our help. It's the same as humans. You and Alpha couldn't do many things when you were little. Now you can. It's about gaining your independence, bit by bit.'

I feel my face heating up. Because what she's said is only half true. It's true for Alpha. She's more independent than any twelve-year-old I know. I'm helpless, like Claw. Sometimes I'm afraid I'll be stuck forever, clawing at a gate to another world. Not because I want it open, but because I'm so scared of what's beyond.

Mum guides us round the rest of the reserve. There are four other wolves in pens, all of them much older than Claw. The rest are roaming outdoors. I notice they don't pay us the slightest bit of attention. They seem quite bored.

'They've calmed down a lot,' Mum says, guessing my thoughts. 'Some of them were skittish to begin with, but now they know there's nothing to be scared of. Soon they'll be out there, living free.'

'How do you know when they're ready?' I ask.

'Well, in here we're tending to almost their every need. They have food, shelter and warmth. In winter, especially, that can make a great deal of difference. When we feel that the time is right, we introduce them to the outdoor enclosure.'

'What if they get cold?'

'That's the thing, Luce. Wild wolves don't live in man-made shelters. They rely on their natural furry coat and their winter layer of fat to keep warm. They find shelter beneath trees and they hunt.'

I know this. I realise I only asked the question for fear she might release Claw before he was ready.

I think back to the wolf in the clearing yesterday, and wonder whether she could have escaped the enclosure. What if she too was scared and lost?

'Have any wolves ever escaped?'

She looks at me, surprised. 'What? No, no. We keep a close eye and we count them every morning.

We'd never try to rewild an animal that isn't ready. If we see a wolf isn't doing well outside, we always intervene.'

'Can we go now?' asks Alpha. 'I'm turning into a block of ice.'

'Yes. Let's get some lunch.'

'Before you go,' Tara says to Mum, 'did you get the email about the visit from the German research team? They want to come in August. They were chasing up because we hadn't replied.'

'What? Oh gosh, no. The WiFi on my phone is so bad around here, they don't seem to be coming through. Thanks for letting me know. I'll reply as soon as I'm on my laptop at home.'

On our way out, I crouch down next to Claw so that our eyes are level. 'You're going to be OK,' I whisper. 'Try to eat. It will make you feel better.' I stroke his head. When I try to describe it to Dad on the phone later, I can't find the words. It was like a warm vibration, an understanding transmitted through a look.

10

Misunderstood Alpha

The rewilding reserve was everything I'm not – calm, ordered, at one with nature. My feet itched to be racing around the court, cold air screaming in my lungs, my breath coming out in plumes.

I could see Mum's eyes light up when she was there, and when Luce met that wolf cub, there was colour in her face for the first time since… since before. So I'd tried to walk around, show interest and ask the right questions, but somehow they turned out to be wrong. And the more I asked, the more I disagreed with Mum. What Claw needed was to be running wild, to feel the blood surging through his veins.

He was rebelling because he didn't want to be imprisoned in the reserve. Who cared about the three steps to rewilding? He didn't, and neither did I.

When I left the reserve, I was two versions of Alpha. Just like when I stood with Luce on the meridian line at the observatory, with my legs in two different hemispheres. Half of me was filled with happy soup, the other with prickly frustration.

Mum takes us to the Treetop Café, run by one of her friends, as a treat. I have to admit it's amazing. We walk up a big staircase, and when we reach the top we're in our own private treehouse, where we're served tea and juice, sandwiches and pancakes dripping in maple syrup. There are special heaters to keep us warm; we need them because of the flurry of snowfall every time a bird moves.

The pancakes we order are small and thick, not like Gra's, which are flat and papery-light, but like the ones Dad used to make for me and Luce. I try not to think about Dad, because this is one of those moments I want to stretch out into infinity and wrap myself up in.

The sun is shining through the treetops. Gra has his eyes closed like a sunbathing cat. Mum chats to Maria behind the counter and Luce casts a glance at me over the table.

I carve a wedge in my pancake and put two blueberries into it. They're my alien passengers.

'Where today, Space Captain Wonder Twin?' I ask, just like I did in our pancake game from when we were little. My pancake is a flying saucer setting off to investigate an unknown planet.

'There's been a new sighting, around Deimos, the second moon of Mars. Let's head over to take a look,' Luce says, smiling.

'Race you!' I say, as I lift my pancake with a fork and make it whizz through the air.

Luce throws back her head and laughs and does the same with her pancake, and our spaceships end up crashing and collapsing into a pool of syrup to be gobbled up.

'Mission failure,' we say simultaneously. For that tiny, tiny moment we're the way we always were. Two hearts beating as one.

The happy day begins to unravel when we get home. As he makes dinner, Gra asks us to gather the wood he's chopped for the fire. I try to put aside the thought we're living in medieval times. There's actually something great about being outside in the snow, as though we're hunters fending for ourselves, battling the elements.

I'm quicker than Luce at loading the logs onto the little trolley that Gra's made from an old wicker basket balanced on top of a skateboard. I get her to pile the logs into my arms to see how many I can carry at once, and we get to six before I can't hold any more. When we're done, Luce sits on top of the trolley load of logs and I pull her. It's the Wonder Twin version of the World's Strongest Man.

We're about three-quarters of the way down the path to the back door, and the rope tied to the basket is rubbing my shoulder through my coat, but I'm not giving up.

'You can do it!' says Luce, and I tell her that I will, obviously, because I'm the World's Strongest Girl – and that's when Mum appears.

She's on the porch, without slippers, and I know straight away something's happened.

'Alpha, can you come upstairs for a second?' she asks, and her voice is like ice. My instinct is to run, but I carefully lift the rope over my head, letting it drop. I feel so light, it's as if I'm levitating. I follow her to the box room that she uses as her study, next to the kitchen. She pulls the door closed and sits in her swivel chair, facing me.

'I got an email from your school, Alpha,' she says in a strange voice. 'Mr Ray sent it more than a week ago, but I didn't receive it until today because of our poor internet connection.'

'Oh,' I say, 'what was it about?' I suddenly feel I'm losing my footing and sit down helplessly on the edge of the armchair, which is covered in books and paper. She turns to her laptop and begins to read.

Dear parents,

Subject: Year 8 Basketball Final

I'm writing to you with the exciting news that our Year 8 mixed basketball team has reached the finals of the inter-school cup for the first time in over thirty years. On Friday at 4.30pm, Jefferson Secondary School will play Everly Academy at the Winston Sports Hall.

We warmly invite you to join us for what promises to be a very close game. Refreshments will be provided. For those of you who haven't previously visited the hall, address details are below.

'Were you playing?' asks Mum, looking intently at me. I know she knows. I nod.

'Did you win?'

I nod again. I should be proud, but my face is burning.

'Why didn't you tell us?' asks Mum in a half whisper, and she looks as though she's about to cry.

The world around me sparks. Dark dots dance in front of my eyes as I stare at the floor. I feel like I'm five years old when Mum caught me telling my first lie. She'd promised Luce and me a lolly if we both finished our dinner. Except then the doorbell went and I quickly scooped the horrible spinach pasta she'd made into the bin, all except a spoonful. When she came back, she was so preoccupied with making sure Luce had eaten enough she hadn't noticed what I'd done and she gave me a hug for finishing it. I began to feel sick even before she opened the bin.

'I didn't want to bother you…' I start, but I know she won't buy it.

'I could have taken time off work. Or if not, Gra or your father would have gone with Lucy.'

A horrible, bitter ball forms in my throat. I shut my eyes.

'Why, Alpha?' Mum persists.

'I didn't want Dad there,' I say.

An awful silence hangs between us.

'He's your dad,' she says finally. 'But fine, if not him, then Gra. And most of all Lucy. You know Lucy would have loved it. She'd be over the moon. You didn't tell her about this?'

I try to swallow, but I can't. I want to scream.

'Don't you understand?' I want to tell her. 'I wanted Luce there. More than anyone. More than you, Mum. More than Gra. More than any of my friends. But you don't know what it would be like.'

I'd played it out in my head.

Everyone's eyes would be on her.

And if Mr Bray was there, well… I couldn't begin to imagine what would have happened. Luce wouldn't cope. And she wouldn't be able to leave because of the commotion it would cause. I couldn't bear it. I couldn't bear any of it.

I don't say any of this aloud.

'No,' I mutter. I pick myself up and slowly walk through the door where Luce is standing, frozen, with an expression on her face that punches the breath from my chest.

11

Heartbroken Lucy

I pull the duvet off my bed and cover myself. It's a little cocoon filled with my hot, familiar breath. I shut my eyes and use Dad's universe technique. It comes from a conversation we once had about Yuri, the first man in space.

I'd asked Dad how far Yuri had gone and whether he'd seen the whole universe. Dad had laughed.

'No way, Lucy. I don't think he would have seen even half a per cent of it. You know many physicists believe it's not actually one universe, but many? They say that Earth is part of a broader multiverse. According to this theory, there are many universes, but they're not connected. They exist next to each other.'

'Not bothering one another?'

'Yes, exactly.'

So I've separated my universes. Alpha can live in the same multiverse as me, but we're not connected any more. We stay out of each other's way.

Even though I use outer space to make sense of what is happening, I still don't understand. Dad had explained that in space there are always triggers for big events. For example, supernovas happen when a star burns through its fuel and begins to cool. This causes it to collapse and explode.

I've searched hard for a trigger for what's gone wrong between me and Alpha. It would be easy to say it was *that* day at school, but I think it started way before.

Sometimes when dark thoughts creep into my mind, I wonder whether it goes all the way back to the beginning.

I remember clearly when Dad told us the story of our birth. We'd been to the observatory for the first time. It was a perfect day. It was wet and drizzly when we arrived, the clouds hanging low and grey over the hill. The weather had kept most visitors away and we'd had the place to ourselves.

Later, when we'd walked through the observatory, seen the Great Equatorial Telescope, the famous Octagon Room, and the meridian line, Alpha ran off down a narrow passageway. Dad started panicking, but she appeared moments later, saying she'd found a secret garden. We followed her down an alleyway that felt like a rainforest, teeming with wildlife.

The clouds were lifting and in that little green patch, sunlight filtering through the trees, butterflies dancing around incredible, exotic-looking plants, Dad said, 'That's our bench.'

'Well, technically it's my bench, seeing as I found it,' said Alpha.

'No; I mean it's mine and your mum's,' he said. 'We came here the day after the second pregnancy scan. I think we were trying to distract ourselves from what we'd found out.'

'You mean, that you were having twins?'

'No, no. We knew that already. It was at the second scan that we found Lucy wasn't growing as expected. You were smaller than Allie,' he said, turning to me. 'And I don't mean a little bit smaller.

You were off the charts small. The doctor was really concerned, and so were we.'

'Why was he so worried?' I asked, a seed of fear sprouting.

'He was mainly concerned that you weren't getting enough nutrients for your little body to develop properly. So I guess it's nothing short of a miracle that I'm here today with my two best ladies and that you're both so brilliant and healthy!'

Alpha rolled her eyes at Dad. She hated it when he called us his 'best ladies', but I felt winded. What he'd said was supposed to reassure me, but the opposite was true. I'd caused trouble and worry for Mum and Dad from even before I was born.

Later that night I went to Dad's study to ask him more about it. He was in the middle of writing a paper on the effect of different lighting conditions on the eyesight of mice, and from his face, I could tell he was at an especially important bit as I'd walked in.

His fingers flew across the keys as he scrambled to get it down. Then he shut his laptop, folding his hands on top to show he was listening, and smiled. 'Lucy,' he said.

'Dad.' I sat in the chair opposite, like a patient in a doctor's surgery. 'Why was I always so small? Even in Mum's stomach?'

He sighed, a crease appearing in the centre of his forehead.

'Nobody knew for certain,' he said. 'The doctor said that Alpha was getting the nutrients she needed. Back then she wasn't Alpha. She was Twin 1 and you were Twin 2.'

'But I caught up?' I asked, and I could hear the doubt in my voice even as I asked the question. Deep down I knew that I never had. That I would always be a bit smaller than Alpha, a bit weaker. I was a piece of space dust. My sister was Alpha Centauri – not one star, but a cluster of some of the brightest stars in the night sky. It was Dad's favourite cluster and I knew, without having to ask, that he and Mum had named her after it.

'Of course you caught up,' said Dad, without hesitation. 'Surely you can see that? It took you a little while, but you did.'

In a way, he's right. There are photos of us from when we are six months old, where she's almost twice the size of me. We look like those babushka dolls that Nanna got us – identical, but different sizes. It must have led to no end of questions for Mum and Dad.

Now I'm only a bit shorter than Alpha; maybe two centimetres. That doesn't bother me as much as the main difference – which is so huge, it has cracked the ground between us.

I would never abandon Alpha the way she abandoned me *that* day at school. I would never, ever be embarrassed of her, no matter what she did or how stupid she looked. No matter what other people said.

As I realise this, the seed of a wish begins to form, and before I can stop it in its tracks, it flourishes. I wish that Alpha and I weren't twins. I wish we weren't even related.

The force of the wish hits me, because I'd never imagined this is what I might want more than anything.

I shut my eyes and try to control my breathing. Then I open *The Secret Guide to the 88 Star*

Constellations, which Dad gave me four days before he told us he was leaving, and I begin to read. I turn the pages without taking anything in. It's only when I see the constellation of Lupus and the image of the tiny wolf among the stars that the darkness retreats, and I can breathe again.

12

Escaping Alpha

I run and run until my muscles are stretched and worn, until my chest aches as if I've swallowed ice, until I no longer feel the blister on my left foot, at the base of my big toe. I run until there's no air left in my lungs, and I'm like a puppet that collapses when you let go of its strings.

I kneel by the side of the road and find there's wetness on my shin which comes away red when I touch it. The gash screams and screams, but even that isn't enough. I put my head between my legs and breathe in to forget, for a moment, what's happened, and it's just me and the tarmac and my rattling heart.

In the pale, dusty light of morning, in a street on the edge of town, I can almost pretend none of it has happened. This is the real world. With streets and shops and schools, and people doing normal things. Gra's house in the woods with the weird old trees and the creepy silence, and the sad wolves trapped in the reserve seem like something out of a bad fairy tale.

The trouble is that according to the map on my phone, there's still over an hour to go on foot, so I direct myself to the nearest bus stop. This time, luck seems to be on my side, because the bus arrives within three minutes. When I'm sitting on the back seat, my head clears. I might not even have to go back for a couple of days.

When we still lived next door, Hector and I were always sleeping at each other's houses, so I figured Mum couldn't be that mad. I'd left a note on her desk to tell her where I was. It was better than sending a message, which might take ages to get through because of the bad signal. My phone buzzes and I wonder if it's her, but it's Hector.

Mum asks if you want dinner?

Yes, please, I type back. My stomach is growling with hunger.

They don't need you, I tell myself, and when the old man across the aisle casts me a surprised look, I realise I've spoken aloud. But I needed to let the words out because I know they're true.

Earlier, when I was in my room packing my bag, I heard Mum in her study. She mentioned Claw, which made my lava pool of anger bubble even higher. How could she keep him in a cage, when all he wanted was to run free?

'Oh, well, that's a result,' she said. 'How did you manage that? Really? She seems to have had quite an impact. I'll have to go and tell her.'

The mystery words could have meant anything, but I knew in an instant and they made my skin prickle with annoyance. She was talking about Luce and the wolf cub. She thought he'd started eating because of her. Suddenly Luce's a wolf whisperer.

I should have known. It's always been this way. Golden child Lucy being praised, praised, praised.

In primary school, Mum and Dad put us in different classes. Dad said it would give us a chance to 'be our own people'. I had no idea what he meant by that, because I was always my own person.

I didn't have a clue how to be anyone else. And everything was great until the time my teacher in Year 1 was ill and there was nobody to cover, so they had to merge our class with Luce's for the day.

Her teacher, who was all big hair and glasses, told us to write about our hobbies. Easy-peasy. Mine were running, trampolining and going to the Dreamery Creamery with Dad (back when we were still friends) to taste ice creams. I'd written 'I like to...' at the top of the page and split it into three sections where I wrote about each of my hobbies and drew a picture. I knew I'd spelled 'trampolining' wrong, but it was an impossibly hard word, and my teacher said that the main thing was to try. I may have also missed an 'n' in 'running', but it was obvious what I meant from my drawing.

Luce's teacher looked at me and furrowed her forehead so hard her glasses fell to the end of her nose. She picked up my paper, and I could see the look of surprise on her face.

'That's not Lucy,' said a boy from her class. Luce was sitting a row in front of me and when her teacher looked at her work, I saw neat lines of joined-up letters. I bet the spelling was 100% and all the full stops were in exactly the right place, and my face burned as if someone had set me alight from the inside.

'You love space, don't you, Lucy?' said her teacher, her voice dripping with so much admiration it made me want to scream.

Luce was the best at school, but somehow she still needed rescuing. She was always the one who Mum and Dad, and Gra and everyone else, ran to. And if something went even the slightest bit wrong, Luce gave up.

What would the world be like if everyone cried and locked themselves away? Who would go to school and to work and make dinner and get on with things? If things go wrong, you have to stand up for yourself.

13

Amazed Lucy

'Alpha's gone to Hector's,' Mum tells me at breakfast, and I feel an immediate surge of relief. Last night I couldn't sleep thinking about what I would say to her.

'You drove her this morning?' I ask, surprised Mum got up so early on a Sunday, the only day she doesn't work.

'No, she left me a note last night,' she says, and I can't read her expression. She doesn't seem angry, more resigned. Alpha knows I know. That's why she ran.

'Anyway, Dee let her stay last night and today.'

I nod and start helping Gra clear the plates. Dee has been Mum's best friend for years. She's one of the friendliest people I've ever met. Even though I'm nowhere near as close to Hector as Alpha, I miss living next to them.

'I need to sort out a problem with the food delivery for the reserve,' Mum says. 'It was supposed to arrive yesterday, but I rang up and there was some mistake with the dates, so I have to pick it up myself.'

'Do you want us to come with you?' asks Gra, concerned.

'No, it's OK. I'll try to be quick. You two enjoy the sunshine.'

'Can I come over later?' I ask.

'Yes,' she says, and I can tell she's chuffed I'm interested. 'I'm told Claw has perked up since yesterday, and I think we might have you to thank for that. He seems to have developed quite a bond with you.'

When she's gone, Gra and I hang out in the back garden where the broken fence is now entirely covered in ivy and a carpet of moss coats the little shed so you can't tell where the garden ends and the forest begins. The air is crisp and brilliant and the sunshine sparkles on the snow – it helps to force Alpha from my mind.

'There are no clouds,' says Gra, 'which means it's perfect.'

'Perfect for what?' I ask.

'Ah, you'll see, you'll see,' he says, tapping the side of his nose. He disappears into the house and I want to run after him, because lately I find I don't want to be left alone. Panic floods my heart and my hands fly to my hair. I try to focus on counting the bluebells, whose heads had just begun to peep out when the snow came.

Gra comes back. His hair is loose today and it billows around him as he walks. He's holding what looks like a battered suitcase. An old, checked picnic blanket is folded under his arm. He wipes the snow off the picnic table and spreads the blanket over it. Then he opens the case, and I'm amazed by what I see.

14

Relieved Alpha

I wake up in Sofia's bed and there are no stupid birds ruining my sleep. Just the comforting purr of traffic and the muffled sound of the TV from downstairs. Sofia's room is covered in manga posters and smells of freshly laundered sheets. She's Hector's older sister and she's in her second term at uni in York, which means I don't need to sleep on the pullout in Hector's room.

Mum called last night. I didn't pick up her calls, but then she rang Dee's phone and I had to speak to her. She didn't seem as mad as I'd imagined – more exhausted and maybe a bit guilty. Serves her right. 'It sounds like Dee is OK with you staying tonight,' she said. 'I'll pick you up tomorrow.' I tried my luck and asked if I could stay for longer. She was about to protest when Hector came up behind me and shouted, 'Please, please, please!' and Mum asked to speak to Dee again. In the end, they agreed that I could stay until after dinner.

I felt immediate relief when I arrived last night. Hector was super happy to see me. Josh wanted me to tell him about winning the final, and Dee gave me a plate of her best spaghetti Bolognese.

When I sat at the table to eat, my skin felt as though it was covered in a crusted layer of salt from my epic run, and I was so tired my bones ached. But I felt light and warm, and soupy inside. Like this was the family I should be part of. The family who really appreciated me. There were no awkward questions, no arguments, no suspicion.

I skip down for breakfast still in my pyjamas and then Vern comes round and we go into the garden for a kick-around. I peep over the fence to see what's changed in our poor old garden, and notice the new patio set and fancy trampoline, and the happy soup in my stomach begins to seep away.

Things get even worse when Vern asks with a sideways grin, 'So, what's the real story? Why did you run all the way here last night?'

My heart plummets. I don't want to tell them, because it will shatter the brilliant day that I deserve to have. But I put the ball on the ground and, sitting down on it, tell them everything – about the row with Mum, about the stupid reserve, about Claw, the imprisoned wolf cub. It swirls out of me like a whirlwind and as the words escape into the cold air, fury rises with them.

When I finish, there's silence, and they both look at me with strange expressions.

'Maybe your mum's sad she couldn't come to the game,' says Hector quietly. 'It could be that, right?'

'You're so gullible,' says Vern, rolling his eyes. 'She's annoyed Allie's still got a proper life here – not out there in the stupid forest. It doesn't fit in with her plan. Parents always have a life plan they're trying to make you follow. And they get annoyed if you're not going along with it – or if other kids are doing better than you. You're never ever good enough...' He trails off and looks up, panicked, as if he's said too much.

'Is that what your parents are like?' asks Hector.

'What? No. I'm just saying generally. Anyway,' he says, turning to me, 'your mum is pretending she's annoyed you didn't invite her, but she probably wouldn't have come anyway. And she'll use this argument you had as an excuse to never come to your games.'

'I'm not sure she's really...' I begin to protest.

'When has she ever driven you to practice?' he interrupts. 'When has she asked about how your games went?'

'I know, but she has her new job and...'

Vern claps his hands together, satisfied. I don't like the smug look on his face, but I have to admit that maybe, just maybe, he has a point. Because, if I think about it, Mum has never once taken me to a coaching session. She doesn't even drive me to school. Since we moved to Whitecastle, she pretends that our old life never existed. I remember how hard I had to argue to stay at Jefferson.

'You don't fit into her life and Lucy does, so

she's chosen her over you. It makes sense if you think about it.'

The more he talks, the more the spark of anger ignited by my argument with Mum spreads through my body. I try to think about the things she used to do for me, but they seem so long ago that they have no effect.

'Are you OK?' asks Hector.

'Of course she's not. But don't worry, Allie. I have a plan to help you.'

I look up at Vern and he's grinning, and he puts his arm around me. For a brief moment, I feel something like hope.

15

Cosmic Lucy

Gra pulls out the cylindrical object nestled in its red velvet case. I take it from him, worrying my unreliable hands will drop it, but it's surprisingly heavy and I grasp it with a strong and steady grip. It has a gold metal centre and a brown leather cover. It's the first proper telescope that I've held.

'This used to belong to my father, Cosmo. Everyone said that his parents must have known what he'd turn out like, because they gave him a very fitting name. All anyone needed to do was add an 's' to the end of it and they'd know what his life revolved around.'

'The cosmos. What was he like?'

'My father was in the Navy and he travelled a

lot. He got this from a manufacturer in northern Norway, where you can see the clearest skies for miles around. He spent some time living with the Sámi. They're indigenous people who live in tents. Their knowledge of the stars has been passed down through many generations.'

'And he gave this to you?'

'My brother and I weren't particularly interested in astronomy, but when my father died, he said to keep the telescope safe. He told me that someday I'd know who to give it to, and I've found that person,' he says, smiling at me. 'What do you know about telescopes, Lucy?'

'They have curved mirrors that gather light from the night sky,' I say, carefully opening the telescope to its full length. 'There are some super old telescopes still being used today. Like the Greenwich 28-inch refractor telescope, which is almost 130 years old. Some of them are huge, like the James Webb one.'

My voice is clear and calm, as it always is when I talk about astronomy.

'Is that the telescope that's recently been sent into space?'

'Yes,' I say, amazed Gra's heard of it. 'Did you know it's about the same size as a tennis court?'

'I didn't. But here's something you might not realise. Did you know you can see the stars even in the daytime?'

'What? No.'

'My father once showed me how to observe the moon from this very spot. The ancient astronomers said the best time to view the moon was during the day. You need to know where to look and you need to watch out for the sun – because through the telescope, it can be almost blinding. Now, if you bear with me, I'll see what I can remember. It's been more than fifty years since I last did this.'

I hand Gra the telescope and he takes a small, dark red cloth from the velvety interior of the case and wipes the lens. Then he checks his watch and positions the telescope above the hedge in the lower left-hand corner of the garden.

'Ah, we didn't have as many tall trees when I was your age,' he says. 'Ideally, you'd be up high, where the view isn't obstructed. But let me see...'

I watch as he adjusts the eyepiece to get the

focus right, slowly moving it inwards while looking through it. The telescope stretches before him and he uses his left hand to hold the shaft steady.

I'm desperate to take a look. I've never seen daytime space.

'Ah, there it is,' he says, after what seems like an eternity. 'Lucy, I present to you the daytime moon.'

I take off my gloves and hold the telescope as if it were the most prized possession on Earth. I position my eye over the eyepiece, and there it is. I want to shout from the sheer enormity of what I see. There are mountains and valleys and crater chains and cracks. I'm looking at another world, a lonely place with no life on it.

'It's magnificent.'

'I'll leave you with the moon, Lucy. I'm going to start making lunch,' Gra whispers, and for once I don't feel scared about being alone.

As I study the blurred border between the light and dark side of the moon, where the shadows meet, I feel a crawl on the back of my neck, and I know it's not the excitement or the cold. I can feel eyes watching me – and they're not Gra's.

I make myself count backwards in my head. *Nine – eight – seven – six.*

A whistle echoes through the trees, then stops. The air is still. Did I imagine it?

It starts again, louder this time, and I realise it's coming from above me. My eyes scan the bare branches. I spot movement.

'Come closer,' says a boy's voice. 'Yes, you. I know you can see me. You in the red coat. Please, it's urgent,' he says.

I freeze. I'm desperate for Gra to come back.

'Come on,' he says. His voice sounds strained this time. 'I need help.'

'W-w-hat?' My own voice escapes in a stutter.

'I've dropped my rope. Can you throw it up to me, please?'

I take a few steps towards the old oak tree at the end of the garden. I see a twist of thick blue rope. I grab it and look up, where a pair of legs in dirty black joggers are dangling down.

'I can't hold on much longer,' says the boy. 'Throw it as high as you can.'

I squat and swing my arms. Before I know it,

the tangle of blue is soaring into the air and I'm certain it's going to get caught on one of the lower branches, but it doesn't. A dirty hand reaches to catch it. I hear a yelp of pain or maybe relief, and – suddenly – there's a boy standing in front of me.

His face is beetroot and his breath is coming out in short, startled puffs, but he's very much alive. He didn't fall.

'Hi,' he says. 'I'm Janus.'

16

Determined Alpha

Vern won't reveal his plan. He says he needs to iron out the details. We press him, but he won't budge.

After lunch, I ask Josh whether he'll take us to the basketball courts in the park and he says, 'Sure, anything for the Player of the Match.' I wonder whether he's making fun of me, but it turns out he isn't.

'Lovely day for it,' says Dee, and she's right. The sky is endless blue silk. It's the brightest day we've had in ages, which is ridiculous because it's May and there should be loads of sunshine, and for a split second I wonder what Luce is up to.

Josh's friends Sohail, Jimmy and Kai come round,

and we go to the courts together. I'm the only girl among six boys (well, technically it's five boys because Hector says he'll watch from the sidelines and keep score), but I don't care.

We see how many hoops we can get in one go, and Josh is incredible. I don't know how somebody so tall can be so light on their feet, and he delivers slam dunk after slam dunk. Twenty-two in a row, and he only gives up because he wants to give the rest of us a chance. I manage nine, which isn't even close to my personal best. I'm mad at myself, but Sohail shouts, 'Way to go!' when the ball teeters on the edge of the hoop and it looks as if it's not going in but does.

We play three-a-side and I'm with Josh and Vern. Hector takes it very seriously and hands out bibs, even though it's a friendly match. We're the reds and the colour matches my mood.

I'm aglow with the fiercest energy. The ball thumps, thumps, thumps against the tarmac in time with my heart. The lines painted on the court criss-cross and I think of us – me and Luce, Luce and me – and the gap that's opened up between us.

The green bibs of the opposing team shift and sway in front of me. I'm aware of them, but I can only focus on the smooth, solid lump that's formed at the top of my throat. I swallow hard, but it doesn't budge.

Then I jump so high my knees crunch from the effort of lifting my body into the air, and I smack the ball right into the centre of the hoop, millimetres away from the frantic grasp of outstretched fingers. It's my best shot ever. I may never do one that good again. Hector's whistle goes, Josh puts his hands up for a double high five, and I feel… nothing at all.

17

Surprised Lucy

'Thank you and sorry,' says the boy called Janus. 'Bit of a miscalculation. It's never happened to me before.'

He's at least half a head shorter than me. He's thin, but his arms look strong and, judging by the number of scratches on them and the layers of dirt beneath his fingernails, he spends a lot of time outside. He's wearing a thin shirt with rolled-up sleeves, despite the cold.

His features are small, apart from his eyes, which are big and blue and crease in the corners. It makes him look like he's smiling even when he isn't.

'Why were you watching me?' I ask.

'Because of the telescope. It glinted at me.'

'Glinted?'

'Yeah. Yesterday I completed the seven-tree course,' he says, and I can hear the pride in his voice. 'I started at the big oak on Welford's Farm and I finished at the pine in front of our house. All I used was the rope. It took me three weeks to work out the footholds and get the positioning right. If you tie the knot too loose, or position it even centimetres away from where it's meant to be, you could find yourself in hot water. Anyway, I completed the course perfectly and then I saw a glint in the distance. Don't tell Dad.'

'I don't know your dad.'

'My dad's Gerry Roski. Your grandpa's known us for years. Why don't you ever come round?'

I shrug, because how can I even begin to answer that question? But he doesn't say anything more. Instead he walks over to the table where the telescope is balanced on top of the case, where I left it.

'You need a tripod, don't you?' he says, and before I can answer, a flurry of words escapes his mouth. 'I can make you one. I'm good at making things. I get it from my dad. He's a carpenter. A tripod is super easy. I can put it together in no time. We need wood from your grandpa but he's always got some going spare…'

'You don't have to,' I interrupt, because it looks as though the word-avalanche might continue forever and a day.

Gra comes out of the house and says, 'Hello, Janus. I see you've met Lucy. Do you want to join us for lunch?'

'Ah, so you're Lucy,' says Janus, 'not Alpha. I thought you were, but I couldn't be sure. I see your sister get the bus to school in the mornings. She wears her hair a little differently to you, and she looks more cross.'

I can't believe he's said that, but Gra laughs and says it's actually a very good summary of Alpha. Janus agrees to join us for lunch, but only once he's run next door to tell his dad.

'I need to be on my best behaviour after everything that's happened,' he says, and Gra nods seriously and says it's probably for the best.

I want to ask what he means, but before I can, he's gone. Then Mum comes home and she's relieved because she says that the wolves will have something to eat now for the next two weeks.

Gra tells her about our unexpected visitor and she's surprisingly interested in meeting him. 'Shall we invite him to visit Claw with us, Lucy? Gra told me that he's into animals.'

My first thought is that this was supposed to be my afternoon with Mum, and I wanted to find out more about Claw to see if I could help him. Plus, spending time with people who aren't my family still seems a little scary. But there's something kind and funny about Janus, the boy who appeared from the trees and can't seem to stop talking.

'OK,' I hear myself say.

18

Strong-willed Alpha

'Right, d'you want to hear my plan?' asks Vern. We're sitting cross-legged in Hector's bedroom after the game, eating Dee's homemade raisin bread. The delicious sweetness fills my mouth and reminds me of when Hector, Luce and I were little and Dee would bring raisin bread to our house every Sunday – until Mum put a stop to it by making us move.

'Go on then. What is it?'

'Allie, I think you need to teach your mum a lesson. You need to show her that she can't just move you to a ridiculous forest far from your friends – just like she can't imprison that poor wolf.'

'What do you mean? How am I supposed to do that?'

'Release Claw.'

'Release him?' says Hector. 'But he's not ready to be released. Allie was saying he's just been brought over from abroad. He probably doesn't know how to hunt yet or anything.'

Vern waves his argument away with the flick of a hand. 'Of course he knows. Every wolf knows how to hunt. It's what he was born to do. We'd make it look as though he broke out. They'd totally freak out that he's gone missing.'

'And then what?'

'That's it. He'll run free and they won't be able to find him. They'd never know it was us.'

Vern's words swirl around my head, like a wind scattering seeds of possibility. I'm almost certain none of them could take root. They're filled with badness, and it's difficult to make something good grow from them – everyone knows that. But one burrows in my mind. I try to stamp it out, but its shoots get longer.

And the same thought repeats over and over in my mind: 'Claw needs to be in the wild. Wouldn't I be doing him a favour?'

19

Gentle Lucy

I hear him the minute we step through the door of the enclosure. A sad, high-pitched whimper. I run to his pen before anyone can stop me.

Claw jumps up when he sees me and lets rip an excited yelp, as if to say *I knew you'd come back.*

His eyes are light yellow and blinking, and there's something in them I can't quite read – perhaps fear, and a little bit of sadness. Without thinking, I stroke the suedey bit of his head between his ears. Then I run the back of my finger along his nose, like Allie and I used to do with Curtains, our old cat, and I can tell he likes it because his whimper turns into a sound halfway between a growl and a purr.

That's when I notice the red marks in the matted fur of his front legs. There, at the height of the lower bars of the gate. When I touch them, Claw whines in pain. They definitely weren't there yesterday. I wonder if he's been launching himself at the side of the gate all night, alone and scared in his makeshift den, where nothing looks like his old home and the darkness seeps into every crevice.

'You know, you shouldn't look him straight in the eye. It'll make him anxious,' says Janus.

'He's not anxious because of me,' I reply, surprised at how angry I sound. 'He's anxious because he's lonely. They found him when he was three weeks old, separated from his mum.'

'That's very young,' Janus agrees, crouching next to me. 'The mother usually stays with the cubs until they're about four months old. He must be feeling lost.'

'He is,' I say. 'He still remembers her smell, and he wishes they could be together again, but they can't.'

Janus throws me an odd look then, and I realise I'm talking a little bit about Claw, but mostly about myself. Because I also feel as though I've lost a parent. He may be at the end of the phone, ready to pick up, saying, 'Luce? How's your day?' but he's not here in person, smelling of peppermint gum, listening to my stories about the constellations I've discovered and telling me who made him laugh at work.

Sometimes I miss Dad so much I feel winded, and the only thing that makes it better is the pick, pick, pick of my fingers against my scalp.

I don't say any of this to Janus, and luckily Mum and Tara appear before he can ask any questions.

Mum sees me stroking Claw and motions for me to back away. 'Don't put your hands in,' she whispers. But she's terrible at whispering and her voice is loud enough to startle Claw, who retreats into the corner of his den.

'His appetite seemed to improve yesterday,' said Tara, 'but this morning he wouldn't touch anything. I gave him the exact same food, so it can't be that.'

She sounds exhausted and fed up. I can tell Claw senses it. That, and the fact all these people are talking about him as if he isn't there.

'Can I try?' I ask Tara.

'How do you mean? You want to feed him?' Mum asks. 'No, Luce, I can't let you. He may look cute, but they're dangerous animals and you haven't been trained.'

'He *is* just a cub,' says Janus quietly. 'He's not going to hurt her. Besides, even if he tried to nip her, how much damage could he really do?'

I could hug him then. I see Tara hesitate and glance at Mum.

'Lucy did seem to have a positive impact on him yesterday. Maybe it would be OK. I'll go in with her.'

Mum runs a hand over her face and looks at me. 'Fine, fine,' she says. 'I hope I don't live to regret this. But you need full PPE.'

Tara explains that it stands for personal protective equipment, which includes a plastic face shield that attaches to my head on a hairband. I worry it's going to mess up my hair, which I've carefully arranged with clips so the bald spots are covered. It seems to be OK though, and besides, everyone is more concerned about poor Claw and what he might do to me.

The blue rubber gloves are pointless, because I've already touched Claw's head with my bare hands and I know instinctively he'd never do anything bad. But I take one look at Mum and know she won't let me in without them.

I follow Tara into Claw's den and crouch down. His tail and ears stand on end. He's excited to see us, and at the same time confused by the strange stuff on my head.

'What does he eat?' I ask.

'He should eat kibble at this time of day,' she says. 'It's similar to dog food. Wolves like meat and raw fish too. We can try giving him some now, if you don't mind the smell.'

We try the kibble, which makes a satisfying rustle.

Claw watches Tara closely and I see his eyes widen. He takes a couple of steps towards the bowl, then hesitates. She steps back and he edges closer, but he won't try the food.

'This is what always happens. And he won't eat even when I leave him to it,' she says, exasperated.

I take some of the kibble into my hand. It feels odd through the rubber glove, like picking up pebbles.

'Here,' I say gently. 'I can tell you're hungry. Do you want to try this? It's tasty. And good for you. It'll give you loads of energy.'

Claw walks up to me and sniffs the kibble. He rubs the side of his little warm body against mine and begins to eat. The handful is gone within seconds and he's already waiting for more. Before we know it, the whole bowl has gone. As I've been feeding Claw, Mum has crept away and come back with a bucket of something that smells fresh, briny and sweet. Claw's tiny snout has picked up the scent and his head turns to see what it is.

Mum hands me the bucket and nods. Inside are raw, cut pieces of fish – probably trout or bass. Gra has told me about the different kinds.

'Now this is a real treat,' I say to Claw. 'Want to have some?'

Claw looks at me with his yellow eyes, and I know he trusts me. He's my friend and I'm his.

20

Furious Alpha

I wait outside Mr Pang's office, staring at the tiled floor that looks like a dirty chessboard.

It's me and Mrs Crystal, the receptionist. I'm annoyed because Mondays are always basketball practice, but today both the hall and the gym are full of parents and teachers and Year 8s. Literally everyone is there, except me. And Mum.

I keep telling myself it's just a parents' evening. I would have hated being there. Whoever thought it would be a good idea to sit next to your parents while your teachers told them how you'd done that term? The clue was in the name. Parents' evening is for parents.

Everyone has a ten-minute slot with each teacher. I'd sent Mum the timetable weeks ago. I'd reminded her again last night when she came to collect me from Hector's. She's already missed the maths session. Soon she'll miss geography.

Maybe she'll still come. I try ringing her, but it goes straight to voicemail. A worry surfaces that maybe something has happened. But she would always be the first to tell us. When she and Dad broke up, she couldn't wait to sit us down in the kitchen to give us 'the talk'. She's forgotten. Or maybe she didn't want to come and couldn't come up with an excuse in time.

'Choc biscuit, darling?' asks Mrs Crystal, coming towards me with a plate. I grab a couple without saying thanks. I know she feels sorry for me.

Out of the corner of my eye, I spot the lost property box. There are some ratty leotards, a pair of shorts, a hockey stick and a tennis ball. I pick up the ball and start bouncing it in front of me. The movement helps.

When Luce and I were little, we went through a superstitious phase. We called it our 'if' game:

'If you reach the end of the garden in five seconds, then Dad will make his special chocolate bombe for dessert.'

'If you can do a handstand without touching the wall, then we won't get any homework for the rest of the week.'

'If you can recite the whole of this poem with no mistakes, then Nanna will get better.'

It's been years, but today I'm playing my own 'if' game. If I can get the tennis ball into the trophy cup on the top shelf of Mr Pang's cabinet, Mum will come through the door. It will turn out that she's been stuck in traffic. I can do it. I know I can. I'm a slam-dunk master. How different can this be from being on court?

I bounce the ball up and down the corridor, trying to get a better feel for it, but I don't have control. The ball is too small and too bouncy. If I want to get it into the trophy, I have to be precise. I keep trying.

Thud. Thud. Thud. I make as much noise as possible, to silence the howl in my chest. It begins to work. The din of hundreds of voices in the hall dies away. It's me and the ball. The ball and me. And the trophy. If I jump, I'll be able to reach the base. I simply need to get my footwork and aim right.

I bounce the ball hard. Adrenaline courses to the tips of my fingers. I know I'm going to score. Luce would know it too, from watching my footwork. She's always two steps ahead.

But the thought of Luce makes the howl in my chest louder. I see her – Luce, with Mum and Gra gathered around Claw, everyone saying how amazing she is with him.

Then, suddenly, I'm not Alpha any more. I'm in Claw's pack and I'll destroy anything that stands in my way.

I ride the energy that surges through me and I'm in the air, my arm in a perfect arc, the small ball above me, and as I land, I can see that I've won. I've won, I've won. I hear the satisfying *thunk* as the ball hits the inside of the trophy. It knocks it over, bringing it crashing to the floor – along with two ceramic plates that were presented specially to our school by a famous potter.

'What is going on here? Allie, what are you doing?'

I'm on the floor. Mr Pang is standing beside me, holding pieces of broken plate. 'Did you throw a ball at these?' he asks, a look of shock on his face.

'Why would you do that? Someone put hours of work into these, Allie. What's got into you?'

'It was an accident. I didn't mean…' I begin to say. In my pocket my phone buzzes. Mum.

'Where are you, Alpha? What's happened? Why aren't you home?'

'Because I've been waiting for you for an hour!' I shout in my head. 'Because I've reminded and reminded you! Because you're always too busy! With your stupid wolves and with Lucy. You have two daughters!'

I say none of this to Mum. Instead, I throw my phone on the floor. I don't want to hear her excuses. The screen smashes, just like the plates, and I think I might feel better, but I don't.

21

Brand-new Lucy

I've done two things today that I would have never thought possible.

The first happened when I was halfway through writing a Victorian mystery short story. Gra had gone to make a cup of tea and found we'd run out of milk. He'd done something to his back when he was piling firewood, and every time he bent over, even a little, it sent a shooting pain down his leg.

'I'll go,' I offered, and Gra was so surprised he turned around too quickly and winced in pain. I ran to help him into his seat.

'Are you sure, Lucy? We can always have peppermint and your mum can get milk on her way home from work.'

'No, no, I'll go,' I said. 'Mum will be late tonight because it's parents' evening.'

Gra gave me the money, and told me to pick up tomatoes and a cucumber too, and I walked out of the door, after he'd told me three times to call him if I needed anything. Gra making such a big deal out of something so small made me embarrassed and even more determined.

But it *was* a big deal. I hadn't been out of the house on my own since the Incident. The shop is a ten-minute walk away. At the end of our street, you turn right, then right again and at the end of a long tree-lined road you're at the corner of the high street and there's Whitecastle General Store. Gra and Mum do a weekly shop at the main supermarket on Saturdays, and Gra and I do a top-up shop here on Wednesdays.

The walk usually passes super quick, as Gra would be pointing out plants or birds, or we'd be talking about something awesome. Lately, he's been telling me loads about his dad, whose telescope I'm now the proud owner of.

I keep it under my bed in its special case, and a part of me is always amazed it is still there in the morning. It seems other-worldly. I've never owned anything so valuable, and I promised Gra I would guard it with my life, which for some reason he found funny.

Today there was no Gra to talk to.

My ears began to tune into every sound that might signal danger. I tried to calm myself by focusing on the birdsong that Gra had taught me about. I could hear the *cheep-cheep* of sparrows, the *sispi si-hi-hi-hi-hi* of the blue tit, the *chak-ak-ak-ak-ak* of the magpie and the *cu-COO-coo* of the collared dove. My boots made little sucking sounds as I walked through the sludge.

Somewhere on a side road beyond the trees, there was the *skrrrrrt-swoosh* of a drive being cleared of snow. They were normal sounds, so why did I feel afraid?

And then it was there – the sound I'd heard before in the car on the way to the reserve: a low, shuddering growl. I broke into a run, sliding through the sludge, my heart pounding in my ears, convinced that any second the incisors of some raging beast would grab my ankles. Somehow, I made it through the door of the shop, where I've been standing for a good five minutes, getting my breath back.

Suddenly, there's Janus. I panic that he's seen me looking flustered, but if he's noticed, he doesn't mention it. He's with a tall, thin, bearded man, and they're both carrying overflowing bags of shopping.

'So we meet again,' Janus says, grinning. 'Lucy, this is my dad. Dad, this is Lucy, Wilf's granddaughter. She's the wolf whisperer.'

I've never been called that before, and I like it.

'Ah, the famous wolf whisperer,' says Janus' dad and his face breaks into a smile. 'I'm Gerry. It's an honour to meet you. Shall we wait and we can walk back together?'

For a moment, I'm worried Gra's told them everything and they're only saying it because they feel sorry for me. Then I remember the growl and I quickly run to get the milk and food. As I wait to pay, everything goes quiet. Maybe they've decided to go without me. My heart speeds up as I push through the double doors, but they're there, waiting, their matching hats pulled tight over their ears.

We have a peaceful stroll back home without any terrifying noises, and Gerry asks me and Gra for dinner. He invites Mum and Alpha too, but I tell him about parents' evening. Mum promised to take Allie out for tacos after, so they won't be eating with us.

'Have you been to the Place of Strength yet?' Janus asks as we're about to turn down the lane to his house.

'The what?'

'The Place of Strength. Your grandpa hasn't shown it to you?'

When I shake my head, he looks delighted. 'Well, you're in for a treat. Dad, can I show her? Just ten minutes.'

'Sure, sure. But I'm making dinner, so it really does have to be ten minutes. No more.'

He takes the shopping bags from us and Janus tells me to close my eyes. The old Lucy would be freaked out, and I'm not sure if it's because of the forest or Claw or the walk to the shop by myself, but I know I'm not her any more.

'Hold on to my shoulder,' he instructs. 'I'll lead. Steady, there are roots underfoot.'

Moments later, I sense the light around us change and I open my eyes a split second too soon, and I can tell instantly we're somewhere special.

To start with, the Place of Strength looks like nothing more than a cluster of weirdly growing trees surrounding some lichen- and snow-covered stones.

But there's something else. It's carried on the gentle wind dancing through the pine needles. It's hidden in the soft carpet of moss beneath my feet and the folds of bark on the age-old trunks, thickened by hundreds of birthdays.

Janus calls it 'the Earth's vibrations'. As I sit there and watch the pinkish dusk creep slowly down from the treetops, my chest expands with it and I know it's something that can't be found anywhere else on Earth.

Janus lifts the back of his coat and sits on a broken branch. He inspects it carefully, to make sure it isn't alive. I like how he is respectful to every living thing.

'Why have you brought me here?' I ask, and my voice is calm.

'In medieval times, people would come here from all over the country to find peace. The first mention of it is in the Chronicles of Whitecastle from the twelfth century. They said it had special healing powers. I'm not sure about that, but I think there's something – something good. It's my favourite place,' he adds quietly. I nod. I can't get my words out, because sharing their special place is possibly the best thing anyone has ever done for me.

We walk back to Janus' house and have a delicious dinner of vegetable lasagne and homemade chocolate brownie with edible glitter. And then I do the second thing that I would have never thought possible, even before the Incident. I climb a tree.

I sit with Janus in his treehouse, which is actually not a treehouse, but more of a platform with a barrier made of rope. My legs dangle over the edge. Below, there's nothing but air and the ground covered with snow. There's a high chance I would break a few bones if I fell from this height, but somehow, I feel OK and my hands aren't even shaking so I don't have to sit on them.

'How do you know so much about wolves, then?' I ask Janus, thinking back to yesterday.

'Millicent,' he says.

'What do you mean?'

'She's an old lady who lives near White Castle.'

'Where near Whitecastle?'

'No, I mean the castle. The village was named after it. It's a ruin – well, it's a heritage site. It was supposed to have been renovated years ago, but nothing's happened.'

'What has Millicent got to do with it?'

'With the castle? Years and years ago, her dad and granddad were the groundsmen there. They had a house on the premises. Millicent lives there. She's a friend of Dad's. He helps her out with odd jobs. There are loads, believe me. Her house is falling apart, but she refuses to move.'

'Why?'

'She's stubborn, I guess. Or maybe she can't imagine living anywhere else.'

'How does she know about wolves?'

Before Janus can answer, a car door slams and a furious voice shouts, 'I do not have to stay here after what you did today. You can't make me!'

It's Alpha.

'I should go,' I say, and the shake is back in my voice. 'It sounds like something's happened.'

22

Outraged Alpha

Next morning, it's double biology and we're learning about genes. I could have done without thinking about my family for a couple of hours after the argument last night, but it looks like I don't have a choice.

'Genes carry information that determines particular human traits,' says Mr Malik. 'They are features or characteristics passed on to us from our parents and our grandparents before them. Can any of you give me an example of a trait?'

'Black hair,' says someone at the front of the class.

'Freckles,' says a boy called Matt, who is new and sitting near me and Hector. 'Even if only one of your parents has them, they're still likely to be passed on. That's what my dad told me. Anyway, I think my kids will definitely have them!' he says, and laughs. His face is so full of freckles it's hard to see where they begin and end.

Next to me, Hector puts his hand up. 'Personality traits, too, like whether you're calm or shy or whether you get angry quickly.'

'Yes, that's absolutely true. Scientists have recently discovered that as much as sixty per cent of our temperament is based on genetics. You've probably heard about the nature versus nurture argument. Studies of twins show, for example, that while there is a genetic component to personality, nurture is as much an influence as genetics.'

'We're not lab rats,' I think, and when everyone turns to look at me, I realise I said it out loud.

Luckily Mr Malik smiles and says, 'Of course you're not, Alpha. I was talking about recent studies in which pairs of twins agreed to be observed.' And he starts drawing the structure of DNA on the board.

Vern's eyes narrow, and that same peculiar expression I'd seen before at Hector's house crosses his face. He seems annoyed on my behalf, and I feel grateful that someone is looking out for me. But my mind flicks back to what Hector said about getting angry quickly.

I remember when we were four or five, Dad used to call me Hot Head. Whenever someone took a toy from me at school, or if Mum tried to stop me from doing something, I would shout and yell and stomp. The unfairness of it all needed a noise. The noise made it better. Dad would put his hands next to my ears and make puffing sounds, pretending there was steam coming out of them.

I couldn't help but giggle and my anger would evaporate with the invisible steam. It didn't work like that any more, and I hadn't spoken to Dad in forever.

Now my anger was a permanent guest and it definitely hadn't evaporated since last night, no matter how much Mum apologised. She'd jumped into the car after the phone call and arrived ten minutes before the end of parents' evening to have Mr Pang tell her about my 'impulsive actions which led to the damage of valuable school property'.

She made some terrible excuse about being held up because of a work emergency, and Mrs Crystal asked whether she still wanted to make the last session which was with Mr Bray, and I put my head in my hands because I didn't want her to speak to him after everything that had happened. I refused to go with her.

When she came back soon after, she seemed confused and worried. Mrs Crystal had gone round the other teachers to gather up my report cards, so we could 'read them together at home in peace and quiet'.

The car journey home was the worst I'd ever experienced.

Mum kept saying sorry, but I didn't believe she meant it. 'I've had a mad day, Alpha, and I truly lost track of time. One of the older wolves we released a couple of weeks ago came back thin and ill-looking and we had to call the vet, but he couldn't come for hours, and Claw has scratched his leg so badly he's got an open wound which we think might have become infected…'

I turned my head to the window because I couldn't listen any more. Mum asked whether I still wanted to go for tacos, and said we could read my report cards together, but I told her I wasn't hungry.

When we were almost home, she asked what I thought of Mr Bray, and the volcano that had been bubbling in my chest since her phone call erupted and I shouted that if she wanted to know so badly, why didn't she ask Luce, who she clearly preferred to speak to anyway.

There was a flicker of shock on her face and she told me we'd discuss everything after I'd calmed down.

'How about we go out tomorrow after school, just you and me?' she'd asked. I told her I was working on a history project with Hector.

When I finally got up to my room, I messaged Hector and told him to ask his mum if it was OK for me to stay round again tomorrow. He messaged back quickly with a thumbs-up sign and a smiley face. So I went to tell Mum in my most matter-of-fact voice, without looking at her. I half hoped she'd put up a fight and beg me to stay. She didn't.

'We're more like our parents than we realise,' says Mr Malik at the front of the class, and I want to shout it's not true, because I am nothing like my mum. I would never forget about one of my children. I would never be so selfish! And I realise my mind is made up.

When the bell rings for break time, I tell Hector and Vern, 'I've decided. Operation Claw starts tonight. We need a plan of action.'

'Are you sure you want to do this?' asks Hector, and there's doubt in his voice.

'Obviously she does,' says Vern, clapping his hands. 'This will be the best decision you ever made, Mickleswick.'

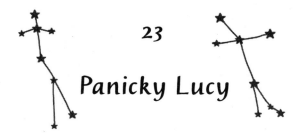

23
Panicky Lucy

Alpha's gone again. Recently, it feels like she's away more often than she's here. So I guess I've got my wish. We're two separate universes drifting further and further apart, only I don't like it as much as I imagined.

I made a pact with myself not to speak to her, but I broke it yesterday when I heard about what happened at parents' evening. I knew how gutted she must be. She's worked so hard – particularly in English – and Mrs Davey would definitely have told Mum how much her writing had improved.

When they got home last night, Alpha locked herself in her room and Mum sat in the kitchen with a cup of tea, her lower lip wobbling. Gra asked her what had happened and as she started talking a sinking feeling developed in the pit of my stomach. I had almost messaged her to remind her to leave work early to get to school for 3pm sharp, but I got so preoccupied with the shopping and going to Janus' house that I hadn't.

'She was so angry about me not coming that she smashed two special plates that had been presented to the school,' says Mum. 'She claimed it was an accident, and Mr Pang said that he didn't actually see it happen, so he let her off with a warning, but I'm pretty sure it was deliberate. I don't know what's got into—'

'It wasn't deliberate.'

Mum looked up at me in surprise. 'How do you know?'

'I just know. Maybe she was bored and practising her moves. Was there a ball?'

'Well, yeah… there was a tennis ball, but that's not the po—'

'See? She was training while she was waiting for you.'

'Why are you so quick to defend her, Lucy?'

'Because she's my twin,' I said, without thinking.

I went upstairs and knocked on her door.

'I don't want to speak to you,' Alpha said. She probably thought it was Mum and not me, but I still didn't go in. I could hear the rage in her voice, and the disappointment, and I knew she needed to be left alone until her volcano stopped spitting lava, and then, when it was done, she'd need a hug.

I went back later, after looking through the telescope to see if I could find Venus (I could) and how many stars I could spot in the constellation of Ursa Major and Ursa Minor, the two bears (ten in total). Alpha liked the two Ursas when we'd seen them in Greenwich, although she said that the Great Bear looked more like a deranged squirrel.

When I went back downstairs, her door was unlocked and she was fast asleep, so I climbed into bed with her and gave her a spoon hug, like she always used to do to me when we were at primary school and I was upset. I knew she wouldn't accept it now if she was awake, and it made me hug her even tighter.

But today she's gone.

'She's doing a history project with Hector,' Mum announces. Her voice is tired and I know it means she doesn't want any questions about it.

Later, when I'm carrying on with the story I started writing for Gra, she comes into my room.

'Luce, can I ask you a question?'

I spin around in my chair to face her, and I can tell it's going to be something bad.

'What do you think of Mr Bray?'

Her question is so unexpected it whips the breath from my chest. Something's happened. I know from the way Mum's looking at me. My fingers move to my head, picking frantically at a few strands of hair behind my ears, but it's not enough.

'He was the only teacher I got to meet in the end at parents' evening,' she says, 'after I royally messed up yesterday. But I didn't like the way he spoke to me.'

'What... what did he say?' I try to sound offhand, but my voice comes out shaky.

'Well, he didn't have a great deal to say about Alpha. He said something along the lines of her keeping up with the work and getting Bs in her homework assignments, which I think is good considering how little effort she seems to put into it.'

I breathe out. Maybe it's a harmless question after all. 'Well, yes – I guess she's getting better at physics,' I say, but Mum ignores me.

'Then I asked about the subjects that they've been working on in class and I told him about the topics Gra has focused on with you. I told him you loved space, and he looked uncomfortable. He didn't want to look me in the eye. Did something happen in one of his lessons, Luce?'

The pins and needles start in the tips of my fingers and toes and spread up my arms and legs. Mum's looking at me intently. She knows that I've found school hard ever since Dad left, but I've never told her about this.

'He's the teacher that took over from Ms Veelam, isn't he?' she continues. 'Did he say something to you?'

I stare at the floor. I wish more than anything that Mum would leave the room. I try to focus all my energy on this single wish in the hope that maybe, just maybe, it might come true.

As it turns out, I have no magical powers. Mum won't budge and I can tell from her expression that she's becoming more and more convinced she's on to something.

I can't answer her question without lying, and I've never lied in my life. So there's a long, sad silence in the air between us.

'If you're not ready, we can talk about it another day,' Mum says, 'but we should talk about it. It will help you, love, even if it doesn't seem like it right now.'

She pulls me close and hugs me tight the way I did Alpha. I never want her to let go.

24

Stubborn Alpha

My tyres keep sliding in the sludge and snow. I left my hat at home and now I feel as though I have icicles in my ears. My battery is about to die on the old phone handset, which I now have to use as a replacement for the one I smashed. Luckily I still have the torch that Hector spent ages sellotaping to the handlebars of Josh's bike. Behind me, a small trailer, which Hector's grandma transported her grocery shopping in, keeps bouncing off my back wheel. We're going to use it to carry Claw. We need to get him far enough away to stop him being found.

A trickle of cold sweat makes its way down my spine. In front of me, Vern curses.

'Come on, Mickleswick. It's got to be somewhere close.'

'All the trees look the same in the dark,' moans Hector, 'and you can't even see the paths on the map. Argh! I went into a branch. I think my eye's bleeding. We didn't bring any first aid…'

'Stop panicking,' says Vern, shining his headlight in Hector's face. 'I knew we should have left you behind. You're too much of a scaredy cat.'

'I'm not!' says Hector, offended. 'It's just awful conditions. I wasn't expecting this.'

'I mean, he's not wrong,' says Vern, looking at me. 'No offence, but why would anyone live in a place like this?'

'Not a clue,' I tell him. 'That's why I'm getting out of here, first chance I get.'

'Hold on, there are some lights up there to the left. Do you think that could be it?'

I check the coordinates on my map. But I catch a glimpse of white fence which I instantly recognise. I get off the bike. My thighs are aching. 'We're here,' I announce.

Hector whips his torch out of his bag and shines it in my direction. I put a finger to my lips. Now we've stopped, it feels like the forest around us has come to life. An owl hoots, there's a rush of wind, and a low howl cuts through the night.

My heart crashes against my chest.

'Is that him?' Hector asks, and I can hear terror in his voice.

'Yeah,' I say, because I'm almost certain that it must be.

'Leave the bikes here, behind the bush,' Vern instructs. We crunch our way up the gravel path. The dark trips me up.

For a moment, I panic. Can I hear voices? It's only Hector, muttering to himself. Mum has mentioned several times there's nobody at the enclosure between midnight and 6am. There are cameras, but I've got the code to deactivate the system, which was written down in a notepad in the drawer of Mum's desk. If Dad was still living with us, he would have told her that you should never, ever write passwords on paper. Mum's memory is almost as bad as mine though, and she relies on that notebook.

You can never be too careful, so I've made balaclavas for us from some old pairs of tights. We look more like comic-book bandits than proper criminals, but I wonder if we might scare Claw more than we need to.

'You definitely remember the code for the alarm, right?' Vern asks.

'Yes, 72319,' I recite, and hold my breath as Vern taps it in.

The alarm beeps twice and the red light turns off.

I breathe out with relief. 'This way,' I whisper.

I ask Hector for his torch to guide us down the corridor, where I remember Claw's den is. I hope Mum hasn't moved him.

Our footsteps echo on the stone floor and we've evidently been heard, because a howling starts up from somewhere within. It doesn't sound like Claw. I think it's the older wolves I saw last time. They sound different – less urgent, more disappointed, angrier. I feel like rescuing them all. It's obvious that what Mum, Tara and the rest of them are doing here is barbaric. Maybe if everything works out with Claw, we'll come back for the others.

Next to me, Hector whimpers. 'I don't want to be here,' he says. 'We shouldn't be doing this.'

'We should and we will,' I insist. I'm a girl on a mission.

There he is. I've caught him in the torch beam, cowering in the corner of his enclosure, his eyes fixed on me.

'You're OK,' I say gently, and he quietens at the sound of my voice. 'Claw, you don't have to be here any more. We're going to release you and take you where you can be free. You won't be trapped any longer!'

I try to sound cheerful, but I'm dreading what needs to happen next. Vern has brought a sack for Claw, but now I'm here, I can't bear to put him in it.

'I'm going to carry him,' I say to Vern. 'He trusts me.'

'Come on, Mickleswick, that's a stupid idea. He's a wolf. He might scratch you or gouge your eyes out. We put him in the sack and then we'll hold it together at arm's length. We'll make a run for the door and the minute we're outside, we'll bundle him into the trailer and cycle down the path. That's the plan. Stick to the plan.'

I'm not listening to him. I open the gate and walk into the enclosure.

'You're safe,' I say quietly. 'You're safe with me.'

His pained animal yelp turns into heavy breathing, and then a soft sound halfway between a snort and a purr. I cradle him in my arms, and for a moment I wonder if I'm doing the right thing. I know nothing about how to look after a wolf. I force myself to remember the reason we're here.

I unzip my coat and fit him inside. As we're walking down the corridor, I sense something in Claw has changed. He's sniffing me closely and his body suddenly arches away from me, startled, filled with mistrust. And the realisation of what has happened hits me. He's figured out I'm not Luce.

He's scratching now, desperate to break away, and I scream at the raw, piercing pain as he claws at my shoulders and face.

He drops to the ground, a fighting bundle of fury. The last thing I see before I drop my torch is Vern grabbing him by the scruff of the neck and bundling him into the sack.

25

Embarrassed Lucy

I replay the Incident in my head word for word. It's a film running on a constant loop in the darkest, most sleepless of nights. It's two days after Dad left. He insists he's only half an hour away, practically down the road, but I know things will never be the same again. I watch as he unsticks his life from ours.

After he's gone, I find three pairs of his socks in the wash basket and an old pencil case with his favourite green highlighters. Bits of himself that he has left behind. I gather them up and put them in a box under my bed.

I'm sitting in double physics, thinking of Dad, when a new teacher comes in. He's much younger than most of our teachers, younger than Mum and Dad too.

'I'm Mr Bray,' he says. 'I'm here to shake things up a bit.'

His first lesson is about black holes, but he doesn't make us do experiments with balloons and aluminium foil like Ms Veelam did, or give out fun fact quizzes.

Ms Veelam's lessons were the only thing that kept me tied together when everything at home was falling apart. But it takes me less than a minute to realise Mr Bray is nothing like Ms Veelam – he doesn't get excited by meteors and gravity and red dwarfs. He doesn't want to bring black holes to life. Instead, he wants us to absorb lots and lots of facts. And he seems to have X-ray vision, because he immediately spots when somebody's not listening and the fingers on his left hand go *click, click, click*. He doesn't say anything, just looks at the offending person, his eyes narrowed, until they stop. His eyes are deep blue and it feels like they're boring into your soul.

Mr Bray's first lesson is about the conditions present on different planets in our solar system.

I love to think about this. Sometimes I imagine myself in my own tiny rocket, hurtling through space to land on Mars or Neptune, or even Saturn, although that would be tricky.

Saturn is my favourite planet because it looks calm and beautiful. There's a scientist who once described it as 'the solar system's seat of cosmic mystery', and I couldn't have put it better. It's made almost entirely of gas, which makes it even more other-worldly. My rocket would go round its rings, but it couldn't land anywhere, because there's no ground.

Alpha's favourite planet is Jupiter, because she says it's the biggest and most exciting. It's dramatic and stormy, with swirling clouds of ammonia, volcanic eruptions and more than fifty moons.

I sit in my usual seat next to Mikki wondering what new things I might learn about Saturn, but then Mr Bray starts saying things that I know are wrong. He mixes up some of the characteristics of Mercury and Venus – saying that Venus has no atmosphere, when I know that it has the thickest atmosphere of any planet. He says that Mercury is the hottest planet, which you might think is true because it's closest to the sun. It's not actually the hottest – Venus is hotter.

And then Mr Bray asks my favourite question: 'Is it possible that life exists anywhere else other than Earth? Anyone want to share their thoughts with the class?'

A part of me is desperate to speak, but something makes me stop.

Ruben puts up his hand.

'I think there are definitely aliens,' he says. 'There have been so many UFO sightings over the years that they can't not be out there. My dad promised to take me on the Extraterrestrial Highway in America and to see Area 51 where they've tested loads of alien technology.'

Mr Bray sighs. 'And what do these aliens look like, Ruben? Green? Three eyes?'

'No,' he replies, and I see he's knocked off guard by Mr Bray's response. 'Nobody knows what they really look like, but I think they're more similar to humans than any of us realise.'

'Who else thinks there is extraterrestrial life out there?' Mr Bray asks.

I feel the hesitation in the room, but I put up my hand. I see Alpha and Hector have too, and a handful of others.

'Interesting. That's almost half of you. The power of stories and fantasy films is greater than I thought. You'll be sad to know that despite these alleged 'sightings', there has never been any scientific evidence that hints at the existence of life beyond Earth.'

This isn't true. It's something Dad and I discussed a lot. Anger bubbles inside me. It's an unfamiliar feeling, threatening to spill over, and I don't know how to deal with it.

Then something happens that I totally don't see coming. I start speaking without even putting up my hand.

'Nothing's been proved,' I say. 'But there have been several studies by NASA that found microbial life forms on Mars and other planets beyond our solar system. And there are other studies taking place right now to look for sun-like stars that have Earth-sized planets in their solar system. I think it's only a matter of time until we find out more about them…'

I trail off, seeing the look on Mr Bray's face. He seems to be finding my explanation funny.

'Well, it looks like we have a scientist among us,' he says.

Mr Bray's stare is fixed on me. I know he won't let me go.

'It seems you know an awful lot about extra-terrestrial life,' he says, smiling at me and opening his arms wide. 'It's only fair you come up to the front and share it with us. I would love to hear more.'

'No, it's OK,' I say. I'm sitting on my hands, but even that doesn't stop them shaking.

'Come up to the front,' he says more firmly, and I stand, even though my legs are jelly.

There's a whisper behind me.

'Luce – don't.'

Mr Bray hears it too. A look of confusion crosses his face as he spots Alpha.

'Ah, there are two of you,' he says, amused. 'And are you as knowledgeable as your sister?'

Out of the corner of my eye, I see Alpha shake her head.

'Alpha is the alpha twin,' Vern says under his

breath so only I can hear. 'You're the smaller copy. Alpha 2.0.'

I shut my eyes, wishing I were anywhere else. Anywhere in the universe except this room.

'Come on,' Mr Bray says again, and I force myself to walk to the front of the room. I stand with my hands behind my back, telling myself not to shake. The shakes don't listen.

'So what else would you like to tell us about aliens?' asks Mr Bray, clapping his hands.

I feel the collective stare of twenty-nine pairs of eyes. It's totally silent, apart from the hum of motorway traffic somewhere far off.

'Nothing,' I mumble.

'Nothing? You had an awful lot to say a minute ago. Well, perhaps you'd like to tell us what you learned about any of the planets today.'

There's a low buzzing in my ears. If I close my eyes, maybe he'll give up.

'Let's start with Mercury,' he says. 'What can you tell the class about Mercury?'

I make my frazzled brain focus. 'It's the planet closest to the sun. It was named after the Roman god Mercurius, who was a mediator between gods and mortals. There have been two space visits to Mercury, in 1974 and in 2004. Its orbit around the sun is the equivalent of eighty-eight of our days on Earth…'

Saying the facts out loud doesn't help, because I hear my voice shaking, and although I'm trying not to look at my classmates, they can see how small, how scared and how pathetic I am. Vern is right. Alpha is the true version of who we're supposed to be. That's why she got her name.

The shakes get worse and the moment I've been dreading comes and I lose control of my body. I can't say anything any more and I feel the trickle of wet down my leg and I muster up the last of my energy to bolt as fast as I can from the room.

26

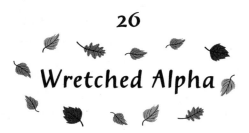

Wretched Alpha

My body feels as though it's been broken into tiny pieces and put back together all wrong. I'm scared of what I'll see when I look in a mirror.

I sit next to Hector, leaning against the shed. Frightened yelps behind us cut through the night. I slap my hands against my ears, desperate to block out the noise. This was not the plan.

Claw fought his way out of my coat, raging against me until he could barely breathe. He had to be put in the sack and tied to the bike trailer with the rope Vern had in his rucksack. Even then, he managed to find his way out again.

He broke free with a yelp and I stopped the bike, shining my head torch in his direction. Next thing, his ears pricked and it was as though a radar had gone off in his head, because he started running at full speed down the path back towards the enclosure.

Vern spotted what was happening and reacted just in time. I'm not sure how he did it, but he managed to get Claw back in the sack.

'What if we let him go and he just goes back to his enclosure?' asked Hector desperately. But I knew we couldn't risk that.

'Wait,' I said. 'I've had a thought. Gra's old allotment. We can keep him there overnight.'

It had belonged to Nanna, and Gra never planted anything there after she died. In fact, all the allotments had been gradually abandoned over the years, and when I frantically shone my torch around, I could tell that nobody came here any more. Maybe, by morning, Claw would have lost his bearings somehow. And we could work out how to release him into the wild.

So here we are. We've bundled the yelping, wriggling bundle of rage into the small, confined space that had, until now, been home to Nanna's rusting garden spades. Vern had tied a knot around an old bolt on the door.

'What now? What now?' demands Hector. 'That rope's not going to hold him in. And I don't want to be sitting here when he forces his way through.'

'It will have to do for now,' I tell him. The last of my energy has sapped away. I'm too tired to speak.

'And what are we going to feed him? We can't just leave him in the freezing cold.'

He has a point. This is something else that we haven't planned for. Claw was supposed to be roaming free by now.

'I'll buy some dog food and cycle over before school.'

'That'll take ages,' says Hector. 'What are we going to tell my mum?'

'You'll have to make something up,' I say, irritated. 'Tell her I had to go home to pick up my PE kit.'

'Are you going to be OK on your own with him? I would come with you but I'm not sure my mum would be happy about it,' he says.

'Come on!' barks Vern. 'He's only a baby. How are you going to help if you're scared of a baby wolf? Stop being pathetic. You're worse than Lucy.'

'Are you serious? Did you see what he did to Allie? She might be scarred for life.'

'At least she won't be *scared* for life.'

Something in me stops when he mentions Luce. It's like an alarm. I won't let anyone speak badly of my sister. But right now, I can't think about her. Everything has gone wrong and I feel like Claw. I want to rage until my breath sticks in my throat.

The only difference is that Claw wants to run back to captivity and I want to break free – free of Mum and Gra, and most of all, of Luce. I want to leave them far behind and possibly never ever come back.

27

Eagle-eyed Lucy

I wake early from a fitful sleep, and my first thought is that the 'morning terrors' have returned. For weeks after the Incident, I would wake between five and six in the morning and not be able to sleep again. My mind would be racing like a 100-mile-an-hour train and no matter how hard I tried, sleep wouldn't come.

I pull up the blind and look out of the window. The oaks and firs are flooded with moonlight. It's a waxing crescent moon, but in a couple of days it'll be a full, glowing orb.

It was Mum's question that made the memory of what happened surface. It's put me on edge. I take out the telescope and distract myself by counting the stars. I go through all the points of the Big Dipper, then Ursa Minor, then Sirius. I'm about to search for the Orion Nebula when I hear the softest of rustles. I pan the telescope down and my stomach lurches. It's the wolf I saw a few days ago. She stands in the clearing, illuminated by the moon, like a creature from hundreds of years ago, when wolves were wild and free. I'm scared to blink in case she disappears.

She's watchful. Her ears prick and she turns her head as if searching for something. I notice a dark red mark by her left eye – a cut, perhaps, or a bite, though she looks too majestic to scuffle with another animal. I shift the telescope slightly to look at her body. She's dark and slender, almost bony, except for her snowy-white snout and the tiny specks of white on her coat, which from a distance look like stars. And then she turns her head, and once again she looks right at me. Her gaze sends a shudder through me.

'What are you looking for?' I whisper, but before I've even finished the question, she's vanished.

28

Strong-minded Alpha

I lie in Hector's sister's room. The sunlight is creeping in through the slats of the blinds. I haven't slept a wink since we got back. I can still hear Claw's howls as we wrestled him into the shed.

I keep reminding myself it was right to rescue him – but I don't feel good about it. I wish there was someone I could talk to. Hector won't let me mention Claw in his house and if I speak to Vern, he'll brush me off. I can't talk to Mum or Luce for obvious reasons, and Gra wouldn't understand.

I pick up my phone and stare at the screen and its alert about Dad's last missed call. For a second, my finger hovers over the call button.

I shut my eyes and try to imagine what he would say. A memory comes rushing back, so vivid, I feel as if I'm there.

Luce and I are about seven and we're on holiday on the Isle of Skye in Scotland. Mum's gone to bed early with a headache and we're with Dad, lying outside our cabin, staring at the sky. Luce is already obsessed with the stars, but I'm more preoccupied by a sign we've seen outside the village pub nearby. It was written in Gaelic and a local man told us it means 'the greatest lesson in life'.

'What *is* the greatest lesson in life?' I ask Dad.

He takes a while to answer and I begin to get impatient.

'To care,' he says eventually. 'To look out for everyone around you, because at our core, we're all the same.'

'What do you mean?'

'Look up at those stars. Imagine how bright they need to be for us to see them on Earth. But do you know what's even brighter? A supernova.'

'What's a supernova?' I ask.

'When a star runs out of fuel, the pressure inside

it drops. It happens so quickly it causes enormous shock waves, which shoot plasma and atoms into space,' he says, and I know Luce is hungrily taking this in.

'Some of them land on Earth, don't they?' she asks.

'Yes, exactly. They nourish our soil and become part of our environment. They also become part of you. Take a look at your hands right now. There's a bit of star there. A beautiful supernova that blew up aeons ago. It's something we all have in common.'

The memory makes my shoulders unclench. I know what I need to do.

'I promise I'll care for Claw until he's ready to be free,' I whisper to the empty room, but I hope that somehow the message has travelled through space like a shooting star and reached Dad.

29

Spellbound Lucy

Janus knocks on the door while Gra and I are in the middle of geography. He's holding a long parcel covered in brown paper.

'It's for you,' he says happily.

'What is it?' I ask, pulling it open.

'Well, I did promise I'd make it and I had a bit of time last night, so...'

It takes me a few moments to realise that it's a foldable stand for my telescope.

I run to the bedroom to get it and we open the stand together. The tripod unfolds smoothly; it has a clamp holder with cushioned lining at the top. Janus adjusts it with a screw to make sure the telescope fits snugly.

'Dad helped me with this part,' he says. 'We wanted to make sure it didn't get damaged, so we used this soft cushiony material.'

'Thank you. It's perfect,' I say. 'Now I can use it to pan across the sky, like a proper astronomer.'

Gra admires Janus' handiwork and eventually ushers me back to the table for geography. 'Janus, would you like to join us today?' he asks, and my new friend nods eagerly.

'Why aren't you at school?' I ask. 'Do you have different holidays here?'

He looks down at the table and I immediately wish I'd kept my mouth shut.

'I'm excluded. For two weeks.'

It's the last thing I'd expected him to say, but I try not to act shocked because I can tell how upset he is.

Gra coughs into his hand. 'It's in the past now,' he says. 'Janus is a stellar student. Now, have you already learned about tides and longshore drift?'

'Not yet, but I know that the moon has a big role to play,' says Janus. 'Millicent told me about it.'

'Ah, Millicent. Send her my regards. I must go

and visit her. How are her Chronicles of White Castle coming along?'

'Slowly, I think, because she puts so much detail into them. She's working on a chapter about the early stargazers now. Actually, I told her you would find them quite interesting,' he says, looking at me.

'The early stargazers,' I repeat, loving the sound of them already. 'Who were they?'

'They're the people who lived here in medieval times. They didn't have telescopes then, but Millicent said they made maps of the stars. Some of these stars had peculiar names. Not the ones we call them. Anyway, she can tell you more if you'd like to meet her. She says you're always welcome. I think you'd get on.'

Meeting new people is my least favourite thing to do in the world, but I'm intrigued by Millicent. I want Janus to tell me everything about her.

'I think you're right that they'd get on,' says Gra. 'Anyhow, you two can have your lunch now, and this is one you'll have to make yourselves. I have a meeting at the village hall. They've asked me to do the catering for their summer party and it sounds like a lot of work.'

'I have an idea,' says Janus, putting a finger in the air, as if he's answering a question in class. 'Why don't we drop in and visit Millicent now? We can make some lunch and take it over to her. We wouldn't stay long.'

'I would normally say you can't drop in on people unannounced, but as this is Millicent we're talking about, I think it's safe to say she wouldn't mind.'

In no time, we've made some cheese sandwiches, and we leave the house with Gra. Except we go in different directions. Janus leads me along the main road out of Whitecastle, but instead of carrying on, as we would to get to the city, he peers down at his feet. I wonder if he's dropped something.

'The grass is too tall. She's going to have to remake it,' he mutters, and then draws to a halt. 'I think we've missed it.' We retrace our steps.

'What are we looking for?'

'The Wolf House,' says Janus, as if it were the most obvious thing in the world.

'You mean the reserve?' I ask, not understanding.

'No, no. Aha! There it is.' He points to a plank of wood on a little pole sticking out of the ground. It's partly obscured by a bush and the tall grass. There's a picture in red paint, which looks like it was done by a child. It's a stick house, with a creature that could be a dog or a goat, and an arrow pointing left.

'It's a wolf,' says Janus, reading my thoughts. 'Millicent isn't the best at drawing. But she always tells me she deliberately made the animal a bit unclear to put people off the scent.'

I look where the arrow is pointing, but there's no road or path. The oaks and birch trees look even denser than in other parts of the forest.

'Is this definitely right?' I ask Janus. 'She lives somewhere here?'

'She does. It's not easy to find, is it? It's her way of making sure that only the people she likes get to visit her. Nobody else would know where to look. From here, I roughly remember the way, but sometimes I still need the signs to help me. The next three are high up in the trees.'

I watch, spellbound, as Janus guides me through undergrowth, round firs and prickly blackthorns. We walk on a bed of pine needles, and our shoes make no footprints. The ground seems to bounce back like a sponge. For a moment, I feel a flicker of fear. If we got lost, nobody would know how to find us. We're like Hansel and Gretel, only without the breadcrumbs.

But the house that appears in front of us is not made of sweets and cake. It's a beautiful wooden structure like an enormous treehouse. It stands proudly in a clearing and is decorated with flower boxes, full of plants of all kinds, many of them looking far too exotic to grow here. Dotted around on the ground are bowls of water and I wonder whether Millicent has many pets, or just a very thirsty dog.

Janus leads me up the stairs to the front door, pulling the chain on a bell that tinkles like a wind chime, and we wait. It's quiet here. Quieter even than at Gra's. It means that every sound is magnified. I wonder if I'm beginning to imagine things, but I'm almost certain I can hear a wolf howl somewhere. It's a deeper, more mature sound than Claw makes, so I'm certain it's not him – and yet it's oddly familiar.

I'm about to ask Janus whether he can hear it too, when there's a patter of footsteps and the door swings open. Millicent is nothing like I imagined. For a start, she's incredibly tall and willowy – taller even than Gra. She has grey hair, cropped close to her head, and round tortoiseshell glasses with thick rims. She's wearing big black boots and a dark-green zip-up suit with lots of pockets, which makes her look like an explorer.

'Ah, is this Lucy?' she asks in a delighted voice, and I can't remember when I've last seen someone so happy to see me.

'Yes, that's me,' I say, and before I know it, I'm being ushered into her wonderful house, as if pulled on an invisible string. I've never been so mesmerised by a total stranger. I gaze around at her home, where every bit of space seems to be extremely well used. The first floor is a single big room with box-like multicoloured shelves running along the walls. They're filled with books, photos, wooden figurines and other trinkets. At one end, in the kitchen area, there are pots and pans hanging on pulleys from the ceiling, and in the corner, there's a huge rack filled to the brim with jars of jam and pickles, and sauces in various shades of red, orange and green.

And then my heart soars, because I notice by the window there's a telescope. It's far bigger than mine, maybe three times the size, and I can tell it's positioned perfectly for stargazing.

Millicent sees me looking.

'So I hear you're an amateur astronomer like me,' she says, bringing us drinks and muffins that smell of carrots and spices. We've already eaten our sandwiches on the way here, but I find I'm hungry all over again.

I nod vigorously through mouthfuls of heaven.

'I'm working on a book about the history of White Castle,' she says.

'Yes, Janus told me – about the stargazers.'

'Ah, the stargazers. What a brilliant name,' she says, shutting her eyes and clapping her hands together. 'You might think of them as an astronomy club from the Middle Ages. I've been poring over historical records that show they used to meet here, near the Place of Strength.'

'How did you hear about them?' I ask.

'It was in some books my father found. He used to be the groundsman at the White Castle, when it was a proper castle. Eventually, it fell into disrepair, and now it's a period property they're renovating for tourists,' she says. 'This house is where he lived when he worked at the castle, and at weekends he would come back to us, to our home in town. It didn't look like this when I first moved in. I had to give it a thorough Millicent makeover. Anyway, my father was helping to clear out the castle basement when it was closed for renovation and he found some very old-looking books. He dutifully brought them over to the estate manager, who took one look at them and said my dad could have them.'

'Just like that?'

'Just like that. I think he had no idea how much they were worth, nor what they were about. They're an incredible mine of information!'

'What else did you manage to find out?'

'Loads. It turns out the stargazers came from all over the country and abroad. They would gather in the castle gardens three times a year, where it was believed the view of the night sky was most uninterrupted, and they would study the stars. They were particularly focused on the constellation of Centaurus. Bear in mind that they were limited in what they could see, because they met back in the 1360s, long before the first telescope was invented. Now, what is your favourite constellation?'

'Gemini,' I say without hesitation. Alpha decided early on it was our favourite, because it clearly belonged to us. Gemini means twins. If you study it carefully, you can see two figures in the night sky, their outstretched arms touching. The twin on the left is lifting a leg, as though she's doing a little jig – that one is obviously Alpha.

'And yours?' I ask.

'Lupus. Constellation of the Wolf. Believe it or not, the stargazers knew about it too.'

'Really? I only recently read about it in one of my books.'

'Yes. You've probably never seen it in the sky because it's only visible from the southern hemisphere. I saw it when I visited my friend in New Zealand. The stargazers had a visitor from the Mongol empire who had seen it too, and he brought them news of it. There's an entry by the leader of the stargazers, which says this visitor was quite confused, because he thought all countries that were home to wolves should be able to see Lupus. This whole area was teeming with wolves at that time. Let me show you something.'

She runs upstairs and returns swiftly with a piece of paper.

It's a photocopy of a basic drawing of a constellation – the dots marking the stars, joined together with faint lines. I can make out the wolf's triangular head, his torso and the curve of his legs.

'Drawn by one of the stargazers,' Millicent says, her voice full of emotion. 'More than 660 years ago.'

The picture is magical. I wonder what it would be like for someone else to find it in many centuries' time.

'I always think the way this wolf bends her head is like my Valentina.'

'More like Hurricane,' says Janus.

I look at them questioningly.

'They're Millicent's wolves,' Janus explains. 'They originally came from the rewilding reserve. She's befriended them.'

There's a sudden buzzing, and I realise it must be Janus' phone. I haven't brought mine with me. He picks it up.

'OK, sure. We're coming,' he says, his eyes wide. He turns to me. 'It's Dad. Claw's gone missing.'

30

Desperate Alpha

I sit in a geography lesson as though I'm floating beneath the waves we're supposed to be learning about. I've had two hours of sleep and I'm so tired my hearing has gone funny. Mrs Vix's voice reaches me, fades, then comes back like the tide.

She gave me a funny look when I walked in late, covered in scratches. I told her I'd had a bike accident and fallen into a bush, but I'm not sure she bought it. The scratches on my face are pink and raised. I know they'll look much worse when they start to scab over. Next to me, Hector keeps shifting in his seat. He's been on edge ever since yesterday, even though he wasn't the one who had to continue the mission this morning.

I set the alarm on my phone to 6am so I could cycle to the corner shop near our old house and buy some dry dog food. I bought some raw fish too, because I knew Claw would like it.

I cycled like mad to the allotments, looking out for signs of Mum, Tara or Gra, even though I knew none of them were likely to be coming this way. When I reached Nanna's shed, everything was still and silent, and my first thought was that Claw had broken out. But Vern's rope was still looped through the rings of the old bolt.

'Hi,' I said through the door as I unlocked it. I didn't want to startle him. 'It's me. I've brought you some food.'

There was an excited whimper on the other side.

I opened the door a crack so I could squeeze through before he pelted out.

'Shhh,' I said, bracing myself. 'I've brought you some fish. You're going to love this.'

There was an earthy aroma in the shed – a smell of nature that had come indoors. Claw sat in the middle, his tail banging against the floorboards, his eyes fixed on me expectantly.

I opened my rucksack and took out two plastic bowls and a plate I'd borrowed from Hector's kitchen. I laid them on the floor. I poured water into the blue bowl and emptied the kibble into the green one. Then I opened the packet of raw fish and started to cut it into strips with the kitchen scissors. The stench almost made me gag, but I made myself keep going.

The entire time I was preparing his food, Claw watched me. His tail had stopped moving and he edged closer.

He sniffed the fish and the kibble, his eyes still on my face, and just as I thought he was about to start tucking in, he took a couple of steps backwards.

I looked at my watch. It was 8.40am already. School would be starting in twenty minutes. There was no way I'd make it in time.

'Come on,' I said, trying to stop my frustration boiling over. 'You have to eat! How will you ever survive in the wild if you don't eat the food that's given to you? And you can't run back to the enclosure whenever you're let loose. That's not the point, is it? You're free! We tried to set you free. You can do whatever you like now. Find new friends, explore exciting lands...'

Hoooooow-ruff!

The frightened half howl, half bark, which I first heard yesterday, was back and I could tell exactly what his eyes were saying: 'You're not Lucy.'

31

Devastated Lucy

Janus, Gra and I hunch over the laptop screen, trying to make sense of the grainy video. It's the recording from the security camera at the front of the enclosure. I'm clutching the scarf I'd given Claw to play with when we met. I'm not sure whether I should have left it as evidence, but it's too late now. I pull it round my neck and feel its soft fibres – it makes me feel somehow closer to him.

Mum is on the phone to the police. Her distressed questions echo along the cold corridor.

'Who would want to steal Claw?' I say. I still can't get my head around it. Until I'd seen the footage, I was certain it was a mistake. I thought maybe Tara had left his gate unlocked by accident and he'd gone searching for food. I felt sure we'd find him, bewildered, cowering somewhere nearby.

Gra rewinds the footage and I stare again at the three figures on the screen, who arrived at the door at 1.34am. They're almost impossible to describe, because they're dressed head to toe in black. They've even gone as far as covering their faces, like the gangsters you see in bank robbery films. One is slightly taller than the other two and is holding what looks like a large bag. They move out of shot and disappear inside.

'Then what happened?' asks Janus. 'Aren't there any internal cameras?'

'There are,' says Gra, 'but they were switched off. Whoever did this knew how to shut down the system. Either that or they knew the code, but that seems unlikely. Only Lucy's mum, Tara and Patrick have it.'

Mum appears in the doorway. I go over to give her a hug.

'The police are coming,' she says. 'They've asked for all the staff to stay outside until they arrive. They want to search the premises.'

'Do you have any idea who it could be?' asks Gra.

Mum shakes her head. 'No idea. My guess would be an anti-rewilding organisation.'

'Anti-rewilding?'

'People who believe bringing wolves back to these parts is dangerous,' says Janus. 'How did they know how to deactivate the system and unlock the door though?'

'Oh, there are all sorts of modern methods,' says Gra. 'You'd be surprised. One of my old clients said he used to put his car keys in the fridge to stop hackers breaking into his car. It's apparently the only place in a building where thieves aren't able to pick up the signal from a key fob.'

'I hope Claw's OK,' says Mum. 'You should go home. I'll let you know what I manage to find out.'

'He'll be found,' Gra keeps repeating in the car. When we get back, he tries to distract us by restarting our geography lesson, but I can't stop thinking about Claw.

Gra can sense we're not fully focused and asks if we could help weed the garden now the snow has melted.

Janus and I get to work, piling up the leafy mulch in the corner and clearing the beds to see what's survived the freak spring snow.

'What do you think actually happened?' I ask Janus.

'I think your mum's right. Claw's been taken by a group of anti-rewilders. They held a protest here when the reserve opened. And they kept writing to the local paper to say it's only a matter of time until their farms and crops are attacked by wolves.'

'Seriously? But wolves don't eat crops.'

'I know. Obviously, most of them have no idea how these animals behave. And now look at what they've done. They've captured a poor creature who's done nothing wrong. They're probably holding him somewhere in captivity, so he's scared witless. It takes someone really brave to stand up to people like that.'

As he's talking, his right hand has formed into a first and he punches it against the open, flat palm of his left. The gesture is so unlike Janus that I flinch, and he jumps. A shadow passes over his face.

'Did you think I was going to hit you?' he asks in disbelief and his arms fall to his sides. 'What has your grandpa been telling you about me? Has he told you I'm violent? Has he said you should watch out for me?'

'What? No. He hasn't said anything like—'

But Janus is in defence mode and all of a sudden, there's a side to him I've never seen before.

'I've got to go,' he says. 'I promised I'd help my dad.'

I want to say something – anything – to make him stay, but I'm so baffled I can't get my words out. By the time I've gathered a sentence together, he's already climbed the stone wall separating our gardens, and landed on the other side with a thump.

'I think you're great,' I say quietly, even though I know he can't hear. 'I want to be your friend.'

31

Roaring Alpha

I check in on Claw again on the way home. I bring some old jumpers I find in the lost property bin, and a blanket someone must have left behind from last year's summer picnic at school. I don't know what wolves like to sleep in, but he might want something to keep him warm.

He's on high alert when he hears me outside, and starts up the loud bark-growl that makes my heart crash against my chest. He backs into the corner of the shed when he sees it's me, sending some rusty garden tools falling to the floor. He's eaten all the fish and some of the kibble, but a lot of it is spilled and I wonder whether he's been throwing himself against the door, desperately trying to get out. I wonder if it's time to try setting him free again, but would he try to go back to the reserve? I need time to think.

'It's OK,' I say, as I try to calmly tidy up. 'I've brought bedding to make you more comfortable.'

He lies down, watching me. When I look up, he's perfectly still. The light has gone from his yellow eyes – the last spark of hope.

I don't know why, but something makes me put my hand out to stroke his head, and the second I do, the growl-bark is back, louder than before. He bares his teeth at me. I can see the glistening grey-pink of his gums and I try my best to be patient, but rage bubbles up.

'Fine!' I shout at him. 'Have it your way! If you hate me so much, I'll leave you here and I won't come back!'

I cycle fast all the way home, my eyes fixed on the empty road. I throw back my head and roar. I keep roaring until my throat stings and my voice comes out in a croak.

By the time I cycle into Gra's driveway, I feel a little lighter, but my body aches. All I want is to tuck myself into bed and sleep, and sleep, and sleep. Maybe, when I wake up, the world might be better.

'What's happened?' Luce asks, opening the door and looking at me in horror.

'I fell off the bike,' I say, not meeting her eyes. My voice sounds hoarse. I've rehearsed the lie over and over in my head, but it feels awful hearing it aloud.

'Your poor face! We need to get you something for that.'

Gra appears and despite my protests, the two of them sit me down at the kitchen table and fetch the first aid box.

'Did you collide with a car?' Luce asks me.

'Yeah, you should see the other guy,' I say, and try to laugh, but it comes out high-pitched. 'No, I skidded and fell into a bush,' I say eventually.

'Why are you cycling, not taking the bus?' asks Gra.

'Josh let me borrow his old bike.' This, at least, isn't a lie. 'I thought it would be fun to cycle, and good for building up my stamina for training.'

'I don't know,' says Gra, looking at me thoughtfully. 'Maybe you should wait until the weather's improved. It's still slushy on the unpaved roads.'

He raises his eyebrow as he's putting the antiseptic cream on, and my stomach clenches. I wonder whether he's suspicious. Maybe he thinks the scratches don't look like they've been made by a bush. I feel too tired to worry about that now.

'I need to lie down. My legs hurt.'

And Luce says that of course I should, and asks whether I'd like a hot water bottle and some of the soup that she and Gra made earlier. She looks me up and down with a worried expression.

I want to tell her that I don't need anything from her. Everything that's happened over the past few months has shown we're better off without each other. But in the end I just nod and make my way upstairs.

33

Astonished Lucy

It's almost midnight and I can't sleep. Upstairs, Alpha's been snoring gently for almost five hours. I'm pretty certain she didn't fall into a bush. She's one of the best cyclists I know, even though she's rejected her brand-new, blue mountain bike because it came from Dad.

Something else is going on. She doesn't want to talk about it, but whatever it is, it's big and it's eating at her, piece by piece. On the outside, she looks like my sister, despite the scratches and bruises, but on the inside, her joy has shrivelled up.

She reminds me of Nanna's babushka dolls which we both loved playing with. Alpha treated them as individual people instead of parts of a whole, and in one of her games the smallest of them disappeared down the drain in our front garden. When we fished her out, a chunk of her head had chipped off and she was covered in dirt we could never quite wash away. Alpha didn't mind – she said it went with her personality because she was a little witch, but I felt sorry for the babushka. To me she looked sad and scared. I hid her inside the other glossy dolls so nobody could see her sadness.

I wonder whether Alpha remembers the game and I'm suddenly desperate to ask her about it, but these days she's not in the mood for talking. When I told her about Claw going missing, she acted shocked, but I could tell her mind was on something else. She turned away from me to show she was done, so I went down for dinner. Mum was taking deep breaths, which she always does when she's trying not to cry.

'Someone's already got hold of the story,' she told us. 'It's going to be in the local papers tomorrow, and who knows? It might even make the national news.'

Gra rolled his eyes. 'I doubt it. Why would that be a headline story?'

'It's a tiny cub who's been stolen from the only wolf rewilding reserve in the country! It's a huge story, Dad. It'll draw attention to the whole argument about whether wolves should be rewilded or not. I could really do without that. We'll have protests outside the enclosure all over again, police everywhere...'

'Well...' Gra began, stirring the bean stew he'd put on the hob. 'Maybe you could turn it to your advantage? Why not contact them and ask to include a message in the article: *If anyone has any knowledge about Claw's whereabouts, please get in touch with the rewilding reserve*, and leave your details, along with a good, clear picture of him. Even better, give a cash reward. People often do that for missing pets.'

Mum ran her hand down her face. 'I guess it wouldn't hurt,' she said. 'I'll see if our trustees would agree.'

I toss and turn thinking about the prize money, and whether it will be enough to encourage someone to tell us where Claw is. I hope he's safe. I picture him, darkness covering him like a blanket, as he howls and howls from fear and hunger and loneliness.

I wish I was brave enough to go out and hunt for him. If Alpha was her normal self, she would know exactly what to do. She would be bold and fearless and make a plan for us both, because that's what she always does.

Ever since we were little, Alpha's had a plan. When we were seven, Hector was tricked into eating spiders by Josh, who was showing off in front of his friends. So Alpha put spiders in Josh's water bottle when he wasn't looking. He'd already swallowed two or three by the time he realised. I bet he still remembers it to this day, even though he and Alpha are friends now.

When Dad had a motorbike injury and was in hospital having a metal plate fitted in his leg and we weren't allowed to visit him, Alpha had an idea. She decided we'd sneak in by pretending we were part of another family, who'd gone to celebrate their grandmother's birthday in the room next door. Although I almost had a panic attack at every turn, the plan worked like a dream.

Even when Mum and Dad started arguing, Alpha knew what to do. Her plan was to try everything possible to make them remember what they liked about each other. She'd whip out old family albums at every opportunity, and make us all relive that time we went on holiday to Greece and Mum laughed so hard at Dad's belly-flop into the pool that she fell in.

One night she even made us cook dinner for the two of them when they came back from work. We'd spent ages, with a little help from Dee and Hector, perfecting the most delicious French seafood pasta, which they both loved. We put on their favourite album of nineties music. Then we went round to Hector's house so they could spend time together in peace and when we came back they looked a little bit happier. Alpha smiled as she gave me our special high five.

'I knew we could do it,' she said, winking at me. 'High five for the twin win!'

Except we didn't win. Not this time. The more I think back to that dinner, the more I realise that's when the old Alpha began to fade away. My bold and fearless Wonder Twin had gone, and I was furious with her, and lost at the same time.

Suddenly, I feel the need to speak to the only person who might know what to do in this colossal mess.

I dial Dad's number, thinking he'll probably be asleep. I get ready to leave a message, but he picks up on the first ring.

'Lucy?'

He sounds so bright and cheerful, it takes a couple of seconds for me to remember he belongs to a different universe to mine now.

'Dad.' I only manage to say one word, and he knows something's up.

'What's happened, Luce?'

I can't hold it in any longer. All the strange and opposite feelings inside me swirl around and threaten to escape, no matter how much I try to focus on the methodic *pick pick pick* behind my left ear, where a clean patch is emerging. And then they all tumble out of me, like wet clothes from a broken washing machine, and I talk and talk and talk at Dad until I've run out of words. I tell him about Claw and Alpha and Janus and how strange and beautiful Whitecastle is, and that I've never felt so comfortable and so terrible in a place at the same time. He doesn't say anything, but I can hear him breathing gently and I know he's listening.

'I don't know what to do,' I say finally. My cheeks are drenched, as I push my wet fringe off my face. 'Alpha would know how to deal with this.'

Dad says nothing for a while, then he asks, 'Why do you think that? Why do you think she would know and you wouldn't?'

'Because she's the first twin. The strongest. You know that. That's why you named her Alpha. The dominant star.'

'We named her Alpha because she was the first to be born, that's true. But she's not the only one with a unique name. Your name comes from outer space too.'

'Lucy? It's the least starry name there is.'

'Perhaps you'll find the opposite is true,' says Dad quietly. 'When your mum was pregnant, I read an article in a journal about a star in the constellation of Centaurus. From the outside, it looked pretty normal, but then scientists discovered something spectacular about it. You see, the core of this star was mostly made of carbon.'

'And?'

'What is carbon in its purest form, Luce? You must remember. I told you when we were in Greenwich, in the observatory garden.'

'Diamond,' I say, without hesitation.

'Exactly. And this star is possibly the biggest diamond ever found. It's a staggering ten billion trillion, trillion carats.'

'But what does that have to do with my name?'

'The scientist who discovered it named it Lucy.'

I'm so stunned by the news, I can barely process it. 'But how have I never heard about it?'

'I was waiting for the right moment to tell you. I wanted to get a strong enough telescope so we could look at it together in the sky. Let me dig something out for you. I kept the journal clipping.'

He shuffles off to search for it and I hold my breath.

'This is what the astrophysicist who discovered Lucy's diamond core said about it: "We have seen evidence of diamonds on Earth... but this is something new, something magnificent. The discovery of Lucy points to the reality of diamonds among the stars." And what do you know about diamond?'

'It's the hardest known material in the universe,' I whisper.

'Exactly. You were so sick in the beginning, and your mum and I weren't sure you were going to make it. You're made of stronger stuff than any of us, though. And when it comes to Claw, you'll know what to do. You don't need Alpha or anyone else to tell you.'

34

Shocked Alpha

'There's been a development,' says Vern, coming over to join us. It's the first time the three of us have been alone together. I overslept this morning and was almost late for school. I didn't even have time to stop off and see Claw on the way, and throughout English he was on my mind. Was he OK? Did he have enough food left from yesterday?

We're on the netball courts behind the science block and I'm shooting hoops to distract myself, while Hector watches. The indoor court we usually play on is being used for sixth-form dress rehearsals, so this is the next best thing. Both the ring and the ball are a bit smaller than in basketball and there's no backboard, which makes scoring a goal doubly hard. I keep trying, but I've only managed to get two out of four.

'What kind of development?' asks Hector, eyeing Vern warily.

'The prize for finding Claw is in the papers today. My dad was talking about it over breakfast. It's £5,000. This is great news for us!'

'How?' Hector asks. I can tell he's nowhere near as overjoyed by this as Vern.

'We'll change our plan slightly. We'll wait another day, then I'll take Claw to the police station. We need to come up with a good story, though. Dad thinks it's the anti-rewilding people who are to blame. So maybe I'll tell them I found Claw near their headquarters. We just need to figure out where that is. I'm sure Dad will know.'

I stop shooting. 'What? We agreed we'd release him!'

'Yeah, and we all remember how that went,' he says, rolling his eyes. 'The best thing now is that we take him to the station. I'll bring him in.'

'And you reckon you'll tell your story and they'll hand over the money, just like that?' asks Hector doubtfully.

'Yeah. You have to trust me,' Vern says, tapping the side of his nose. 'I'll give you your fair share.'

'What does that mean? If anyone gets any money, it should be Alpha. She's the one who told us about Claw. She could use it to pay the fees for the Bayville Basketball Academy.' Hector's eyes narrow.

'I don't want any money—' I protest, but Vern cuts me off.

'This plan was my idea,' he says firmly. 'Neither of you two wimps would have done it without me. You'd be too scared to touch the vile little creature. You probably think he's super cute, even though he's vermin.'

'He's not vermin! He's a powerful predator,' protests Hector, and his hands form into fists.

Vern laughs. 'He doesn't look much like a predator to me.'

'Well, he's practically a baby. He wasn't really given a chance, was he?'

'Believe whatever you want to. All I know is

you wouldn't have done it without guidance from a master.'

'Master of lying, more like,' spits Hector.

I listen to them. There are two facts about the boys I thought were best friends that smack me with full force.

For the first time ever, Hector isn't looking up to Vern. He isn't intimidated by him either.

But the even bigger realisation is about Vern. He's not who I thought he was. He's not a friend helping me decide what to do about Whitecastle, Mum and Alpha. There's something broken inside him. Something he's kept hidden, that has managed to slip out. A damaged, dirty babushka doll with a glossy exterior.

Fury rips through me like a tornado. I need to sit to steady myself.

'How do you see the money being split?' Hector asks coldly.

'I hadn't really thought about it,' says Vern. 'I reckon I should get half, and you and Allie get a quarter each. It seems fair, for the amount of effort put in.'

'I see. And what are you planning to spend your share on?'

'It's none of your business. Let's say I have plans.' There's an edge to Vern's voice that cuts the air like a knife.

It's obvious he needs money for something important. I'm going to find out what, but for now I park the thought. I have much bigger things to deal with.

35

Brave Lucy

I repeat Dad's words over and over in my head all the following day. In the morning, Mum leaves us with the instruction to stay home in case the police arrive with news. She goes to the reserve to make sure the animals are safe and to oversee the installation of a new security system.

She's standing on the porch with her bag on her shoulder, and I can tell she's bracing herself for the journalists and protesters she might have to face. Mum is the second bravest person I know, after Alpha. I feel guilty at my relief that she has moments of fear too.

She's back in the early afternoon, which is just as well, as I haven't been able to focus on any schoolwork. My mind keeps flitting back to Claw.

I know I should be doing more to help. So when Mum asks whether we might join the small search party she's assembled, I agree straight away.

'We can't get more people to join, sadly,' she says. 'And I can't spare too many of the team, as they need to look after the other wolves. Tara and Sam will come with us.'

'What about Gerry and Janus?'

'I rang Gerry earlier. He's working on a project for Millicent Fenchurch. I think Janus must be with him. They said they might be able to help tomorrow if they finish early. We'll ask Alpha when she's back from school.'

I imagine Janus at Millicent's house and wish I could be there with them, away from the panic and worry.

We break up into three search parties: Sam on his own, Mum and Tara, and Gra and me. We take the area immediately north of the rewilding reserve, near the Place of Strength.

'It's pointless, isn't it?' I ask Gra the minute Mum is out of earshot. 'Whoever's done this has probably packed him off and driven far, far away.'

The image of Claw yelping in the back of a van fills my head and hot tears spring to my eyes.

Gra notices and pulls me into a hug. 'Lucy, nothing is pointless if you're doing it for someone you care about,' he says. 'Plus, it's not easy looking after a wolf in a house or flat without arousing suspicion. If your mum is right and it's a local protester who took Claw, we might find he's being kept somewhere closer than you think.'

We spend two or three hours scouring the area. We go along the main road leading into Whitecastle, checking the bushes on either side. I stay close to Gra – even though this area is now familiar to me, the trees are so dense it's easy to get lost. We keep calling Claw's name and listening for the smallest telltale sound, but there's nothing.

We walk to the Place of Strength, and I tell Gra that Janus brought me here.

'It's one of my favourite spots in the entire world,' he says. 'I usually come here alone to be with your nanna. She's in every leaf around here. Sometimes when it's very quiet, I hear her voice carried on the wind.'

I squeeze Gra's hand. I imagine that Claw would like it here too, but he's nowhere to be seen. Then Gra takes me through the cricket fields, and across the pitch we see a white building with peculiar-looking old-fashioned chimneys.

'Whitecastle School,' he says. 'It's where Janus goes, and where your mum went many years ago.'

Most of the kids have left for the day, but a few are still spilling from the gates, and as I watch, I find that I don't feel scared. Maybe it's because this looks completely different to our school in town.

I wonder what Janus could have done that was so bad that he's been excluded.

As we walk along the main path through the forest, an elderly couple pass us. The woman is barely taller than me, and she's wearing a straw hat. The man is in overalls and is pushing a wheelbarrow with a mountain of cabbages. Gra gives him a smile and a wave. They don't return his greeting.

'Enemies of yours?' I ask Gra.

'Claudia and Jack Welford. They're not my enemies. At least, not until this wolf business. We used to be close friends. We spent almost every weekend together after your grandmother passed away. But they decided their beliefs were more important than our friendship,' says Gra. Even though he's calm, I sense he's upset.

'They were first on the picket line when the reserve opened, even though I tried to have a frank discussion with them about it,' he says.

'Where do they live?' I ask.

'Over there. They run the farm behind the Place of Strength.'

Gra and I spend another hour searching then, deflated, we head home for dinner. Perhaps the others have found Claw, but the look on Mum's face when we get back tells me all I need to know.

'We can grab some food and head out again,' I tell her. 'Where's Alpha? Can she help?'

'She says she's not feeling well. She's gone to bed. And thank you for offering, Luce, but I don't think there's any point doing anything else tonight. It will be dark soon. What we really need is help from the police. I hope we'll get it tomorrow. They'll have better search methods and more people.'

As I lie in bed, thinking, I'm doubtful. A big rescue party with police dogs is only likely to scare Claw. I remember how he leaned into me, how he let me stroke his suedey head. If he heard my voice, I know he would react. He'd give me a sign that would lead me to where he was. Dad's right, I know what I need to do.

I change into my old jeans, T-shirt and hoodie. I take my school backpack from the bottom of the wardrobe and creep downstairs. I can hear Gra's snores as I carefully navigate the creaking stairs. My hand shakes as I clutch the banister, but there's something stronger propelling me forward.

I tiptoe into the kitchen, grabbing a bottle of water, a packet of biscuits and a couple of apples. I open the drawer by the sink, where I know Gra keeps his torch. I put it in the bag with the food. And then I stand on the doorstep, just like Mum did this morning, breathing deeply.

Is this the bravest or the most stupid thing I've ever done? I know that if I don't do it, I'll never forgive myself.

36

Frightened Alpha

I'm bounding towards the hoop, the lights of the stadium reflecting off the floorboards. The excited chatter of the crowd bounces off the curved walls and echoes. My opponents try to get the ball. They attempt to steal from all angles, but I dodge them.

I'm super Alpha, flying through the air like a tiger queen, and I haven't come this far not to win. It's my first match at an international stadium, and all eyes are on me.

'Look at that girl,' says a hushed voice. 'She's not even thirteen and she thinks she has this in the bag!'

'Who does she think she is?' someone else responds. 'Who let her in anyway? It must be a mistake.'

There's laughter. It sounds like it comes from a young child. It grows in volume. Other people join in.

I ignore them. I'm on a mission. I concentrate on nothing but the ball.

My tactics work, as I leave my opponents behind and my path ahead is clear. There's nothing standing between me and the hoop. This is it. This is the moment I will show all the doubters what I'm made of. That I deserve to be here.

All that remains is to draw my energy down to my feet and tell them to make a giant leap towards the hoop, which is the most important hoop I will ever have to shoot through.

As I begin to soar on that perfect arc with the ball balanced in my hand, I'm distracted by a creature on the court. A small, furry, frightened creature whose legs are sliding on the polished floor. He's howling, and as my head turns mid-jump, I see his eyes are fixed on mine. He wants me to help him.

I force my focus back on the hoop, but it's too late, far too late. A groan escapes from me and the ball falls from my fingers and hits the ground with a deafening *thud*.

I'm shaken into consciousness by a noise, and it's a while before I realise I'm sitting bolt upright in bed in my room at Gra's house. My heart is crashing madly. But it isn't the nightmare that's woken me.

I heard a noise, a *creak-thud*. Someone is walking around. It's probably Gra on one of his midnight toilet trips. There's something unusual about the sound, though. I can't put my finger on it.

I listen again, but other than the whistling of the wind outside my window, the world is quiet.

37

Bold Lucy

The night is pitch black, except for the dusty glow of moonlight. An owl hoots and there's a scuttle in the trees.

I fumble with the torch, worried that I didn't check the batteries, but to my relief it switches on immediately. The beam is feeble in the darkness. I remember Dad's words when I first told him how petrified I was of the dark: 'Think of it as a blanket that the world throws over itself when it needs to tuck itself in for sleep.'

A plan has half formed in my head. There's very little to it, but it's the best I have. It involves the Welfords. I remembered what Gra told us about them.

'They'd pitched tents and waited all night for the

team to come and cut the ribbon,' he'd said, outraged. 'They had a food stall and everything. People were playing instruments. And then the chanting started. *Keep the wolves out! Disgusting vermin! They'll destroy our farms!'*

I imagine Claw caged somewhere on their farm. They were probably the type to make up a story about how he'd appeared from nowhere and started attacking their animals. Maybe they'd already sold their story to the papers and everyone would read about it tomorrow.

I try to calm myself, to think where Gra said their farm was. He'd mentioned the Place of Strength, so I head in that direction.

'You can do this,' I repeat in my mind. *'End of the road, turn left towards Janus' house and then it's the first turning to the left between two old oaks. You have light. You're OK.'*

I was prepared for darkness, but not for the incredible sound filling the forest. It seems to be louder when the world is invisible. It's unsettling.

There are chirps, rattles, whistles and trills. When I listen harder, I hear drumming somewhere above my head. I recognise all these now as bird sounds, but at night they seem louder, stranger, almost ghostly. Cautiously, I step forward. There's a single streetlight outside Janus' house which tells me I'm on the right track. I know I have to turn left here, but I'm dreading being submerged in the forest.

If only I had someone with me. Dad, or Alpha, or Mum, or Gra, or Janus. My feet refuse to go further and my hand flies to my head to find the comforting patch behind my left ear. I start to pick away at it. I can't do this. I thought I could, but I can't. There's a burning shame inside me, mixed with panic, but the panic is winning.

Then Claw floats into my mind and I realise my nerves are nothing compared to what he must be feeling. I imagine him howling for help, and that's enough. I walk forward. The Place of Strength must be close now, and I tell myself that as soon as I reach it, I'll be safe. I speed up.

I find my route through the bushes and the clearing emerges in front of me. It's flooded in a dull silvery glow. At first I think it's moonlight, but I realise with a start there's someone there. The silhouette of a person sits on a tree stump in the centre. I'm so stunned I drop my torch. *Thump.* I fall to the ground, my fingers scrabbling to find it. The person – whoever they are – has stood up and they're coming in my direction.

'Who's there?' they ask, and even in my panic, I'm relieved to recognise the voice. It's Janus.

He reaches me and I see he has a head torch, which casts the pale silvery glow.

'Lucy?' he asks, shocked. 'What are you doing here? It's half past midnight.'

I'm so glad it's him I don't stop to think he might still be angry with me, and I give him a huge hug.

'Are you OK? What's happened?' he asks, concerned.

'Nothing. I mean… nothing new. I decided I couldn't sit around at home when Claw might be suffering somewhere. I need to help find him.'

'So you've come into the forest in the middle of the night?'

'I should have done something sooner, but I was too scared,' I admit. 'I know it sounds ridiculous, because it's pitch black and all I have is Gra's torch – which as you can see, isn't that helpful – but I thought Claw might be at the Welfords' farm. They've always been against the reserve and wolves. Gra told me. I thought I'd investigate.'

In the pale light he looks surprised and even mildly impressed.

'I'm sorry,' I say. 'For – you know – thinking you were going to hit me.'

'It's OK,' he replies, and motions for me to follow him to the tree stump to sit down. I begin to relax, looking around properly. This place is even more beautiful by night.

'Will you freak out if I switch off the torch for a second?' he asks. 'I want to show you something.'

'Go on.'

'Look up,' he whispers.

When I do, the view takes my breath away. The inky sky above is littered with stars, and I don't know why, but they seem brighter, clearer and more magnificent than I've ever seen them before. I can see the North Star, Ursa Major and Minor, and so many others without needing a telescope.

'The reason I was so upset when you flinched that day,' says Janus, 'is because I did hit someone. It only happened once, and I still can't believe I did it. I hit a boy in my class called Oscar who I won against in football. It was a fluke, really, but he didn't like it and said I'd cheated even though I hadn't. When I protested, he said, "I bet your mum would be proud. Oh, wait..." and that was when I hit him.'

'That's horrible,' I say.

'I know, but I couldn't help it.'

'No, I mean what *he* said was horrible. Awful, in fact.' Gra had told me that Janus' mum had died at the end of last year.

'It was,' Janus agreed. 'But I shouldn't have hit him. What's worse is that I hit him pretty hard. I guess I didn't know my own strength. I broke his nose and he ended up in hospital. He's fine now. It was scary when it happened, though. There was so much blood. That's why I was excluded from school.'

'I'm sorry.'

'My mum used to love this place. When I was younger, she'd collect me from school and we'd come here before going home. Every day was different. We'd count the birds we could hear, and try to identify them. If it was good weather, we'd sit for a while and talk about what happened that day. We'd check on our tree…'

'Your tree?'

'Yeah, look – it's this one,' he says, switching the torch back on and directing the beam towards a thin trunk. 'It's a horse chestnut. We planted a conker together on my fourth birthday and I'll soon be twelve, so it's almost eight years old. It outgrew me two years ago. The leaves are starting to bud. When we finally get some proper spring weather, it'll look a lot more impressive. Mum said this was probably the year it would be taller than her. But, well… we never got there.'

'You must miss her very much.'

'I do. She'd been sick for a long time, though. I don't miss seeing her sick,' he says quietly. 'I mainly miss talking to her. She was always full of good advice. If she was here, she'd know exactly how to help us find Claw.'

'Maybe we can work it out together. At least

we can try,' I say, determined, remembering Dad's words.

'We can and we will,' says Janus, putting a fist in the air like a superhero. 'I think you're right. The Welfords' farm is the best place to start. But they have an Alsatian – Charlie. We'll have to be super careful not to wake him. He's old, but his ears are still good.'

'OK, where do we go?' I ask. With Janus next to me, I feel infinitely braver.

'The entrance to their farm is a bit further along the road that my house is on. I think going around the back would be safest. We might jump over the fence there. Hold on to my elbow. I'll guide you.'

Janus lowers his beam – I'm guessing so it doesn't wake Charlie – but it makes it almost impossible to see where we're going.

At first the ground underfoot is solid, but we soon enter a bushy area and I feel twigs bending against my legs. They snap under our feet, but I can't be sure if it's us making the noise or some invisible creature whose territory we've stumbled into.

'Watch out for your hands. There are loads of nettles here,' Janus whispers and I pull them into my coat sleeves. Eventually, we reach the fence.

'It stretches all the way ahead of us,' says Janus. 'Probably for another twenty metres. Let's follow it and see if we can get in around the back.'

I do as he says, although my jeans get caught on brambles sticking out of the ground like natural booby traps. At one point I trip and almost go flying, but steady myself on a tree trunk.

By the time we reach the spot Janus is aiming for, I have scratches all the way up my legs. He shines the torch against the wooden fence, which is old and dark. Parts have rotted away. Janus tests the planks with his feet, but they don't budge.

'I thought there might be a gap somewhere,' he whispers, frustrated, 'but I can't see any. It looks as though we're going to have to jump over it.'

I'd been preserving the battery of Gra's torch, and I use it to search for a tree to climb. There's only one close enough to the fence, but it looks spindly. Janus examines it too.

'You go first,' says Janus. 'That way I'll be able

to help if you can't get over. And I'll be right behind you the entire time.'

I heave myself up onto the first branch. It bows under my weight, but I keep climbing. When I'm level with the top of the fence, I dare myself to shine the torch into the farmyard. I can see several pens, and the back of the Welfords' house.

'Tuck the torch into your coat,' Janus instructs. 'Reach over to your left. You should be able to pull yourself up. There's a coop on the other side. You can lower yourself onto its roof and jump to the ground.'

I want to tell him it's easier said than done, but the branch I'm sitting on is bending ominously, so I wriggle forward and somehow, miraculously, land on the roof of the coop with a *thud*. Squawks emerge from inside. I wait, frozen to the spot, but nothing more happens.

I jump to the ground and I'm grateful to see Janus following a few seconds after.

In the glow of his head torch I can see that the chicken coop is one of three, all presumably filled with sleeping birds. We peer into each, though they seem an unlikely place to hide a wolf. As expected, there's no sign of Claw. We explore the farm, making as little sound as possible. In the biggest pen, I quietly call Claw's name as Janus shines the torch in all directions. A couple of disgruntled pigs peer at us through half-closed eyes, but there's nothing suspicious.

Through the sheep enclosure at the far end, there's another shed, and I nudge Janus towards it. There's a small movement inside and my heart soars. But when we peer through the window, we see a single goat sleeping next to a large tabby cat.

'He's not—' I begin, then a short, sharp bark shoots through the air like a bullet. Next to me, Janus spins around and his head torch catches a dark, furry shape running between the pens, straight for us. At first, my frazzled mind thinks it could be a wolf – then I realise it's Charlie, the Alsatian. He barks again, this time louder, closer, more ferocious.

'Run!' shouts Janus, and he grabs my hand. I can't remember which chicken coop we'd landed on when we arrived, so I climb the first one I can see. I can hear Charlie panting behind me. Lights turn on in the house. This is all going badly wrong.

Janus pulls me onto the roof and scrambles around to find the tree.

'This isn't the right place. I can't see the tree.'

He groans.

The unmistakable sound of voices is coming from the house. 'Charlie? Where are you?' a man bellows. It's Mr Welford. 'What have you found?'

'There's no time. We have to jump to the ground.'

'From the top of the fence? It's too high. We can't.'

'We have to,' said Janus, desperation in his voice. 'I'll go and you follow.'

My heart is a drum as I watch him leap over the edge, merging into the blackness lapping at the fence like an unknown sea. I'll have to launch myself into it too.

'Are you OK?' I ask, but there's no reply.

'Oi! Who's there?' barks Mr Welford.

I hesitate, close my eyes. And jump.

38

Lightning Alpha

I wake up to Gra's voice.

'How are you feeling, sleepyhead?'

'Better,' I say, although I'd woken several more times after I'd heard that peculiar sound. I'd listened for it again, but all was quiet. Still, I feel on edge. I haven't seen Claw for ages and I'm desperate to know how he's doing. He's spent more than twenty-four hours by himself in the pitch-black shed. I'd left him enough food yesterday, but he's probably going mad from loneliness.

'If you get dressed super quick, you can have a bagel to eat in the car and I'll drive you.'

'What? No, no. It's fine. I'll take the bus as normal.'

'I'm pretty certain you'll miss it, Alpha. You've already had a couple of lateness notes, and we don't want you getting into any more trouble.'

I stare at my alarm clock, which for some reason hasn't gone off. I must have forgotten to set it. Gra's right. There are six minutes until the bus leaves. I won't make it. And he won't let me cycle. Not after I'd told him my injuries were from a bike accident.

My brain can't come up with any excuses, so I accept the lift. In the car, I avoid talking by telling Gra I need an extra power nap.

When we arrive at school, I think about waiting for him to drive off before heading back to see Claw, but I don't know how to get there without my bike – there's only one bus per hour.

Besides, Vern has already clocked me in the playground and he's beckoning to me.

'Today's the day,' he whispers, before we've even said hello.

'The day for what?' I ask, but I sense what's coming.

'We're taking him to the police. Look,' he says, 'the perfect injury.'

On the back of his calf there's a red half-moon. I can see the individual teeth marks – in a couple of places, they have drawn blood. It looks much too realistic to be drawn on.

'Where did you get that? Did you see Claw? I told you I was checking on him!'

'Well, I'm glad that I did go, because it seems that you're not doing a particularly good job!'

'What do you mean?' I ask, dread rolling over me.

'He's completely trashed the place, hasn't he? He's a violent, horrible little runt. They all are. Just look what he did to me! I'm with the protesters. Wolves should never have been brought back to this country.'

'What did you do to make him bite you?' I ask, and my voice is thunder.

'Nothing – I was trying to defend myself! I took him some food, which I wouldn't have done if I knew how he'd react. He totally went for me. I had to take extra precautions. He's so vicious I thought he might eventually break the door. It looked like he'd been going at it for hours! Stupid animal.'

'You tied him up?' I shout, and a couple of kids turn around to look at us.

'Stop being so loud. You'll jeopardise the mission.'

'What mission? We were supposed to set him free!'

'I know, but it looks like that's not possible, doesn't it?' he says, eyeballing me. 'So we may as well do the right thing and turn him in. Besides, it's you who wanted to take him in the first place, so I don't know why you're pretending it's all my fault.'

That final sentence practically winds me. Because Vern is right. I never said no. I never once tried to stop the plan from being put into action. Instead, I helped make it happen.

My hands hang uselessly at my side.

'So that's final,' says Vern with a knowing smile, which I'd always thought was confidence, but is actually a mask that tricks people into following his lead. 'It doesn't feel good when someone else is better than you at something, does it?' he says. 'You're not so in control now, are you, Player of the Match?'

'Maybe I have a plan,' I say, but I don't sound convincing.

'If you do anything, I'll tell the police it was your idea. Hector will back me up. They'll have no reason not to trust me. In fact, it will all make sense to them. How *you* managed to disable the alarm, how *you* knew exactly where to find Claw. And once I tell them, it will make your mum's reputation even worse than it already is. Maybe it's the reason they need to close down the stupid rewilding reserve.'

'You wouldn't do that.'

'Who's going to stop me?' asks Vern. 'You and your pathetic sister?'

I take two steps towards him. We're so close our noses are almost touching and I can see a magnified red hill of a spot that's beginning to form above his right eyebrow. He's so shocked he doesn't move.

I spit out every word.

'You – do – not – call – my – sister – that!'

'What is going on here?'

It's a voice I know all too well. The mocking tone could only belong to one person. I turn to face Mr Bray.

'I see you're having something of an altercation with Vernon, Alpha.'

'He called Luce pathetic!' I shout.

'What was his reason for saying that?' he asks.

My mouth flies open. I can't believe the question. From the corner of my eye, I spot Hector. His arrival sparks lightning inside me.

Looking at Mr Bray now, a new realisation hits me. I wasn't there for Luce when this teacher, who we were supposed to trust, humiliated her in front of the entire class. I didn't stand up for her, just as I didn't stand up for Claw in front of Vern. Now these two bullies are ready to take me down. It's not going to happen.

I clear my throat, as a crowd gathers around us. 'Is there ever a valid reason,' I say, loudly, 'for one pupil to call another pupil pathetic, Mr Bray?'

His eyebrows shoot up. 'Alpha, context is everything,' he snaps. 'Surely you're bright enough to know that?'

'Maybe I'm not,' I say. 'Tell me. Tell *us* what you mean.'

'We all know that a struck match will not light in a vacuum, for example,' he says calmly, but I notice something in his expression, which shows that he knows he's overstepped the mark, and he's aware of everyone watching.

'I'm not sure everything can be explained with a science lesson,' I reply. 'And I would argue there is absolutely no context that makes it OK for Vernon to call my sister pathetic.'

I see Vern open his mouth, and I wonder whether he's going to follow through with his plan of dobbing me in. He must realise he'd be revealing his own involvement too, as he shuts it again quickly.

'Let's discuss this at break time,' Mr Bray hisses. 'You're late for class.'

I spend the whole of our morning history lesson thinking about what to do. All I'm certain of is needing to get to Claw before Vern does, and there's only one way I can do that. Our classroom is well positioned to see the main road.

I pass Hector a note under the table: *If I run out of the room suddenly, tell Ms Hedges I'm feeling sick and have gone to the toilet.*

When I notice the bus at the top of the hill, I dash – hoping beyond hope that nobody is looking out of the window. I don't stop until I'm standing on the bus that will take me back to Whitecastle.

39

Hopeful Lucy

I walk groggily downstairs, trying not to put weight on my right ankle. I wince, remembering the shooting pain in my leg as I pelted through the forest after Janus. When I'd jumped from the top of the chicken coop, I'd landed awkwardly. But there'd been no time to think about anything. We had to get away from the Welfords. It was only when we were safely on the main road that I dared to look. In the light of the torch, I saw my right ankle was huge – almost twice the size of the left.

'You need to pack that in ice when you get home,' Janus had said, leaning down to examine it. 'Does it feel numb or tingly?'

'No, just painful.'

'It's probably not broken then. If it gets worse, tell your mum or grandpa. Put ice around it and it might be better by morning. If not, we can ask Millicent what to do. She knows lots about healing injuries with plants from the forest. I also think she's our best bet if we want to find Claw. I don't know why I didn't think of it sooner!'

I need to persuade Gra to let me visit Millicent with Janus, and make sure he doesn't notice my ankle.

But it's silly to try and hide anything from Gra. His intuition runs deeper than the roots of the Emperor of the South.

I'm pretty certain I've hidden my swollen ankle and scratches under my pyjamas, yet Gra says, 'Something tells me, Lucy, that today will not be a day for learning.'

How does he know?

'I was actually going to ask whether I could go and see Millicent,' I say truthfully. 'Janus seems to think she can help us find Claw.'

'I hope he's right. Your mother's worrying herself sick. And there's panic in the village this morning. Apparently there was a break-in at the Welfords' farm. They couldn't see whether it was a person or an animal, but obviously they're saying it was wolves.'

'What? They think it's Claw?'

'They didn't say Claw specifically, but people think it was a wolf from the reserve. Go and see Millicent, Lucy. I hope she has ideas for what to do. We'll catch up on your schoolwork later. I'm going to join Tara and your mother in the search.'

I'm careful not to walk around the house in front of Gra, so he doesn't spot my ankle. But when he leaves, Janus comes to collect me and together we set off for Millicent's. The swelling is better, but it still hurts when I put weight on my leg.

This time, I know all the signs to look out for and I help Janus locate the arrows in the trees. Millicent opens the door to us with a cup of something delicious-smelling cradled in her hands. She's wearing green, as always.

'Ah, you've come. Still no sign of him?'

Janus shakes his head. I realise Millicent must have been getting updates on Claw from Gerry, who has been fitting more bookshelves for her over the past week.

'What happened to your ankle?'

We sit in her kitchen and she makes me take off my shoe. It's nowhere near as big as it was last night, but there's a spreading purple bruise stretching from the sole of my foot to above my ankle.

Millicent moves my foot up and down and side to side. I wince, but the pain has lessened slightly since yesterday.

'It's not broken. Just a bad sprain,' she says, confirming what we thought. 'May I ask what happened?'

She listens, her eyes becoming wider and her mouth curving into a smile as we tell her about the Welfords running after us.

'I would have liked to see their faces,' she admits. 'But, still, you shouldn't have done that.'

'I know... we're getting worried something terrible has happened to Claw, though.'

It's only when I say it aloud that I sense I've been squashing this fear somewhere inside ever since Claw went missing. I've been convincing myself I needed to be brave, but now I feel hot tears springing to my eyes. There's a strong chance he isn't safe at all.

Millicent pulls me close. I breathe in her smell of earth and leaves and the rich spice she uses in her cakes.

'I'm not sure I can be of great help. I know somebody who might be, though. I don't suppose you have anything of Claw's? Anything he liked to play with? A collar? They have collars at the reserve, don't they?'

I shake my head, frustrated. 'Claw did have a collar, but I think the police have taken it for investigation.'

'Hold on,' says Janus. 'Didn't you give him your scarf to play with? The one you're wearing now?'

'I did. But why would it be any use?'

'Could I borrow it?' asks Millicent.

I hand the scarf over.

'Come with me,' she says.

She takes us to the clearing outside her house which is like part of her garden, the edges blurring into forest. We sit on a bench between two apple trees and she puts her fingers to her lips, letting out a shrill, high-pitched whistle.

We sit for a couple of minutes. I hear the wind in the fir trees.

From nowhere there's a flash of white among the green. A long snout, a white beard, a magnificent arched back covered with white specks. It's my wolf – the wolf I've seen in Gra's garden. She's here now, inches from me, and I don't feel even a prick of fear.

'Hello, Valentina,' says Millicent, and she puts out her hand in the same way I did to Claw when we met.

Except this is an adult wolf. She's wild and free. She hunts for her own food, and answers to nobody. Yet here she is, edging towards Millicent's hand. The closer she gets, the more clearly I see the markings on her back. They're not oval, as I'd thought. Some of them appear to have spiky edges, like stars.

Millicent catches me looking. 'That's why I named her Valentina – after the first woman in space.'

Valentina's snout is now in Millicent's lap. She shuts her eyes as her human friend strokes behind her ears.

'I have a job for you,' she says. 'For the two of you.' I look up to see another wolf, bigger than Valentina and darker in colour, with white-rimmed eyes. I guess this must be Hurricane. Both wolves cast a glance in our direction, but they don't seem bothered by us. Their special bond is with Millicent, nobody else.

'A cub has been lost. One of your kind. There's probably some scent of him left on this scarf,' says Millicent, looking at Valentina and Hurricane in turn.

The wolves sniff at the red wool, and I watch, fascinated.

'Did you know wolves have an incredible sense of smell?' she asks. 'They should be employed by the police instead of dogs. The olfactory centre in a wolf's brain – that's the part responsible for their sense of smell – is huge. It's about the size of my fist, whereas in humans it's no bigger than a pea.'

'Do you think they can smell Claw's scent?'

'Well, they're having a good sniff of your scarf, so I think there's enough of his smell left. Wolves have special scent glands near their tails and, believe it or not, each wolf has a unique smell.'

The wolves move away from the scarf and seem to stand to attention with their ears pricked. Valentina looks at Millicent, her head cocked slightly, as if asking what to do next.

'Have a little nibble for your troubles,' says Millicent, taking something out of her pocket. I realise it's the same kind of kibble we used to feed Claw.

'See if you can sniff him on the wind. We'll follow you.'

They seem to understand completely. Valentina takes a few steps towards the house, sniffing the ground, then the air around her. Hurricane goes after her, and we follow close behind.

The wolves hesitate. Valentina moves left and Hurricane to the right. Maybe we're too far away from Claw, or maybe his smell on my scarf isn't strong enough.

Then they both face the same direction – the route we'd taken to get to Millicent's. In a burst of speed, Hurricane bolts ahead, Valentina hot on his heels.

'Quick!' shouts Janus, and despite my burning ankle, I'm already running.

40

Agonised Alpha

The second I jump off the bus at Whitecastle, I run so hard the cold whistles in my ears and the breath threatens to stop in my chest. I need to keep going. I hope nobody saw me pelting across the playground, but even if they did, they won't know where I've gone. Only Vern will know, and he'll come after me. There's a good chance he's already on his way.

I haven't been to the allotment in the middle of the day before. It looks more derelict and lonelier than ever.

I slow down in front of the shed and listen for a howl or a whimper, but there's no sound. Panic pulses in my chest as I untie the rope holding the door. That's when I see it. Under my knot, there's a padlock that wasn't there before. Presumably only Vern holds the key.

'How dare you!' I scream. I hear a scuttle inside the shed, followed by a familiar bark-howl. It's quieter than usual and a little hoarse. I realise Claw's probably been howling for hours.

'Claw, I'm going to get you out,' I say. 'There's an obstacle I didn't expect, but I'm going to do it.'

I check my bag for something to cut through the padlock, but the best thing I find is a lizard-shaped keyring, which won't even make a dent in it. I need a plan B. I try to wrench the rusty bolt away from the door, where nails are coming loose, but no matter how hard I pull, it refuses to budge.

The howl continues, but quieter still, as if he's on the verge of giving up.

'I'm here, Claw,' I tell him. 'I'm not going away until I get you out. The door's not going to work, so we'll have to try something else.'

I walk round the shed to see whether there's a broken slat or anything that might give an escape route for Claw, but frustratingly, it seems pretty sturdy.

I notice a chink in the window. It's high up on the back wall and possibly too small for Claw to get through, but it's my only hope. I take my jumper off and wrap it around my hand. I've seen this done before on the crime dramas that Dad watches. You need to protect your hands. I search for the closest big stone I can find. I need to be careful the glass doesn't land on Claw and cut him, and that he isn't too startled by the noise. It seems a ridiculous thing to think after trapping him in a shed for three days.

I finally find the perfect rock. It's heavy and has a ragged edge.

'Claw,' I say, keeping my voice steady, 'we need to let you out and I can't do that without breaking the window. Sorry about the crash you're about to hear. Try to keep calm, OK?'

There's no sound from inside, but I know I'm running out of time. There's an old wooden fruit crate leaning against one of the other sheds and I use it as a step. I stand on tiptoe, shut my eyes, and punch the glass.

I must have hit the window harder than I imagined, because I hear a shower of glass raining down and a frightened yelp.

'Don't worry,' I shout, forgetting to be quiet. 'I'm coming to get you.'

I wrap the jumper tight around my fist and put my hand through, feeling for the latch that will open the window. Ignoring the shard of glass that's pressing into my wrist, I twist. The rusty lock gives and the window swings open. I pick away as much of the remaining glass as I can and pull myself up.

Luckily, the window is bigger than it looks from below, and I can squeeze through. Claw is quiet. He watches me lower myself down and comes closer to have a sniff. Now I know what he's doing. He's testing to see whether I'm Lucy. Our voices are similar, so it's only when he smells me that he realises I'm not the good twin. He throws himself wildly at the intruder, who is also the person who put him in this prison. Me.

'Shhh... I'm here to get you out. I'm not going to hurt you. I'm going to lift you up to the window and you're going to have to jump. D'you understand?'

He doesn't. When I try to get hold of him, his teeth close around my arm. I manage to dodge at the last moment. 'Listen! Why can't you *listen*?'

He backs into the corner of the shed. A beam of sunshine illuminates the cramped space, bouncing off the shards of glass, glints of light dancing across the dirty walls.

Claw's beady eyes lock with mine. His teeth are bared and he lets out a low, steady growl like a train engine that's about to whirr to life.

'I hear you,' I say. 'I hear you and I see you. I would be the same. Maybe even madder. You have every right to hate me. I'm a bad person. The worst.'

The low growl continues and I'm running out of ideas.

'Claw, look up at that window,' I say. 'There's freedom. Luce tells me there are all sorts of species of bird, and flowers you've probably never seen, and trees that are almost 500 years old with peculiar names. There are other wolves – your kind. Fresh air, adventure and millions of things to discover. In here, there's dust and glass… and me. Outside, there's the whole world waiting. All you need to do is jump.'

He doesn't move. What else can I do? I have to show him. Suddenly the window seems extremely high up. But jumping is something I'm good at. It's all in the curve of the ankle, the bend of the knee. 'Elastic knees', as Dad used to say. I pull my hands down like a skier to propel myself through the air, and I imagine a huge, coiled spring under each of my feet. I push upwards with my legs, and I soar.

My fingers grasp at the ledge, and my feet slam against the wall, as I try to heave myself up. I grab at the window frame. Then I feel a cold, sharp slice of pain and my left palm is soaked with red. Even so, I have a strong enough hold now and I pull and pull, ignoring the numbness that is beginning to spread through my hand, and suddenly I'm up on the ledge. I feel sick.

'Come on up,' I say to Claw, but my voice sounds distant, echoey. I don't know if my vision is blurring, but he's looking at me with a mixture of worry and confusion. 'I know wolves can be incredible jumpers. You're only small, but you have it in you. If I jump down on this side, will you come after me?'

I stare at the blood that is gushing between my thumb and forefinger, and my head feels as if it's being lifted by a helium balloon. I need to jump down before I fall. Right now.

I land in a heap outside, and stare at the sky. It's a brilliant blue, scattered with a few wisps of cloud. Luce would remember the name of that type of cloud, but I don't.

It feels good to lie here, taking a rest from the world. I shut my eyes and drift. But I can't rest yet, not until I hear the *thud* of four small paws on the ground next to me.

Finally, after what seems like an eternity... there it is.

41

Watchful Lucy

Valentina and Hurricane have caught a firm scent and their legs carry them, swift and strong. I'm surprised at how fast Millicent is too. She's like a creature of the forest herself, blending into the background in her camouflage gear.

I try my best to ignore the pain in my ankle and follow Janus, who deliberately lags behind a little to keep me company.

Every few minutes Valentina stops to sniff the air and check she's on track. Sometimes she subtly adjusts her course and then carries on. The more certain she is, the more my heart soars with hope. I try to be realistic. Maybe she only knows where

Claw's been? Maybe he's left his scent somewhere and that's what she can smell?

We're at the main crossroads now leading out of town, and she takes a left, towards Janus' school and the cricket pitches. She hesitates at the edge, looking at Hurricane as if to ask him what to do.

We catch up with Millicent. 'They don't usually leave the forest unless it's the dead of night,' she whispers. 'I guess they know the quickest way is through the fields, but it leaves them exposed. Wolves never want to be seen.'

She places a hand on the back of each wolf. 'I know you wouldn't normally do this, but it's important,' she tells them. 'There's nobody around. If you dart over quickly, not a soul will know you were here.'

Valentina flicks into action. Her left leg moves forward slightly. She's understood. Suddenly she races off, so fast none of us, except Hurricane, can keep up.

There's nothing for it but to run after them – Millicent in the lead, then Janus and me on my injured ankle. Halfway across the field Janus sees me struggling and turns back to help. He puts his arm around my waist, and we do our own version of a three-legged race across the field.

'Come on, we can't lose them,' I say, willing my legs to go faster.

'We won't,' says Janus, and I look up to see Valentina, Hurricane and Millicent waiting on the edge of the forest. They've slowed down now they're out of danger, but they are as agile and poised as ever.

'I think we might be close now,' says Millicent. 'Look, their tails are standing to attention. They've got a strong scent. Careful, though. There's no path and there are brambles everywhere.'

We keep going, following the wolves through a part of Whitecastle Forest I've never been to before.

Through the trees I hear a lonely, desperate howl – and I know exactly who it belongs to. I would recognise it among the densest chorus of animal sounds. It's Claw. The howl is more urgent than I've ever heard. A plea for help.

I push in front of Janus and Millicent, but nothing prepares me for the sight that awaits us.

Claw isn't tied up and he doesn't look hurt. But he's running madly around a body that's lying on the ground, splayed out like a starfish.

The second he sees us, he launches himself at me, clawing at my legs and howling, then running back to the body.

I fall to my knees, not daring to go closer.

There's a pool of red by the left side of the person. Their face is half covered by a navy jumper, but a few locks of hair emerge like coiled snakes, and a scream escapes me when I see they're the exact same shade as my own.

42

Returning Alpha

There are piercing white lights everywhere. I'm back at the Chase Centre Court in San Francisco. I'm standing beneath the basket and there's a beeping sound above my head which I haven't heard before. It must be the beginning of the victory celebration, because the crowds are shouting my name. *Al-pha, Al-pha, Al-pha*. We've either won the NBA championship or I've beaten a record, because I've never heard support like this. If only I could remember what I've done to deserve it.

The more I listen, the more I'm aware of a particular voice in the crowd. It's very similar to my own and it's somewhere at the front of the stands. I search among the masses of people, all looking the same in their caps and hoodies. Someone touches my hand and pulls me into a warm embrace.

'You're here,' she says. 'You're back.'

I open my eyes. I'm not on the court at all, but in bed, in a stark white room with people staring at me – familiar faces. Mum, Dad, Gra. They look concerned, but they're also grinning at me encouragingly. I can see Dad is trying to say something, but I can't make out the words. There's only one voice I'm listening for, and when I turn to my left, I see her looking back at me with eyes identical to mine, and that's when I know I'm going to be OK. Luce is here and everything else will somehow fall into place.

Three months later

43

Excited Lucy

The knock on the door comes sixteen minutes earlier than I expected, but I'm ready. I'm wearing a brand-new red school shirt and a dark-green jumper that itches a bit at the neck. There's an energy fizzing through my veins from my heart to the tips of my fingers. It's not anxiety. It's vibrant and happy – like a song.

I remember Dad's words on the phone last night: 'Luce, I have a good feeling about this. You're a shooting star that's finally landed in the right galaxy.'

I swing open the door and burst out laughing, because Janus is standing there with his ironed shirt and immaculate dark-grey shorts and he looks nothing like what he really is, which is wild and untamed.

'What? I can be presentable if I try,' he says, offended. 'Plus, this might not be nearly as clean if we go you know where en route.'

'You two are eager to get to school,' says Gra, smiling. 'When I was your age, I always left it until the last thirty seconds before the bell went.'

'It's good to be early on your first day,' says Janus, not looking Gra in the eye. 'You know, to get the lie of the land.'

'Oh, the lie of the land, of course,' says Gra. He winks at us. 'When you put it like that, it makes sense.' As always, he knows much more than he ever lets on.

'Enjoy it,' is all he says, then he watches us run out through the front garden and take a left turn onto the main road that leads to Whitecastle School. It's the same route that Alpha always takes to get the bus and the same route that Mum used to take all those years ago, when she was our age. As I walk along it, there's no tremor or pull of anxiety.

Janus assures me there's no Mr Bray equivalent at Whitecastle.

In fact, there's no Mr Bray at Jefferson Secondary School either. It was Alpha who encouraged me to tell everyone what really happened. I was sitting on the edge of her bed in hospital two days after we'd found her and Claw at the allotments. She'd been drifting in and out of sleep, her poor left hand in so many layers of bandage she looked like she was wearing a white boxing glove. We'd taken turns sitting with her, but this time when she woke up, it was just me and Dad.

Her eyelids fluttered open, she drew a breath and suddenly, she said that she was ready to talk.

'To the police?' I asked.

'To them too,' she said. 'Mainly to you both.'

And she told me about the guilt that had been crushing her ever since that day with Mr Bray.

'Alpha, don't worry about it now. You need to rest,' Dad protested, and I realised this was probably the first time they had spoken to each other since he'd left. Once Alpha started talking, she didn't want to stop, though.

'It sounds stupid when I say it,' she admitted quietly, looking at me, 'but he was so rude and impatient. I realise now he picked on you because you knew some of the things he was teaching us were wrong. Even *I* started to notice it, although my space knowledge is nowhere near as good as yours.

'He told us the other day that the Hubble Space Telescope is the largest telescope ever invented, but everyone knows that's not true and that the James Webb Telescope is both bigger and more powerful. Well, maybe not everyone... but *I* know, because you told me.'

'You remember that?'

'Of course,' she said. 'I remember everything you teach me.'

Her words floated around me like a hug and I felt as though our universes may have just come back together.

'I think I should have a word with this Mr Bray,' said Dad. 'I really don't like the sound of what you're telling me.'

'You should!' said a voice from the corner of the room, and we turned to see Hector. I didn't know how long he'd been standing there, but Alpha's face lit up when she spotted him.

'He deserves to be put in his place,' he continued. 'And you kind of already did in the playground, Allie. Everybody saw.'

He told us exactly what happened, and Dad's eyes widened, then narrowed. 'That settles it,' he said. 'I'll make an appointment with Mr Pang.'

When Dad came back from seeing Mr Pang, he told us that whatever Alpha had said to Mr Bray that day in the playground had obviously been very powerful, because quite a few students had told their parents about it, and some had already made complaints against him. Dad's visit had been the final straw. Only a few days later, Mr Bray resigned – before he could be dismissed.

Alpha asked whether I'd come back in the autumn term, but I'd already made my decision. I was going to Whitecastle School. There was a week left of the summer term, which was the perfect time to meet everyone ahead of the new school year.

From the moment I arrived at Gra's, I realised I was never made for the city. I belonged with the ancient trees, with the wind that howled through the ruins of the castle. I was one of the stargazers exploring new universes in the Place of Strength. Like Claw, I was slowly being rewilded.

'Here we go,' says Janus, checking his watch. 'We have exactly twenty-five minutes before school starts, but maybe we'll get lucky.'

Millicent's house is beautiful in the sunshine, and the air is filled with the sweet fragrance of the many blooming flowers in her front garden. I've decided that in the future I want to live in a place just like it.

We're waiting for her to answer the door when Janus puts a finger to his lips and whispers, 'Listen.'

I tune in to the sounds of the forest, and then I hear it. It can only belong to one wolf.

We creep slowly around the side of the house, careful to talk at a normal volume. Claw still isn't good with loud noises, so the more warning we can give him, the better.

And there he is – poised mid-bite, his ears alert as he listens to the familiar sound of our voices. I'm struck by how much he's grown. He's about twice the size he was when I first met him. His fur is darker, his snout is longer and he can run at high speed.

He's been in the wild for almost a month and he's thriving. He was released much sooner than Mum expected. She's certain that Valentina and Hurricane are teaching him to hunt.

'They came to find him,' said Millicent when she saw them together. 'He must see them as his protectors.'

Now they've formed a miniature pack and mostly hunt on their own, but they like to come to Millicent's back garden whenever they need an extra bit of care. She occasionally moans about how demanding they are, but I know she wouldn't have it any other way.

Today, Millicent, Valentina and Hurricane are nowhere to be seen. It's just us and Claw. We've realised he likes coming to the garden in the mornings, but he isn't here every day, so we're in luck. It's as if he's been waiting to wish me a good first day at school.

He's sometimes a little unsure as I approach, because it takes him a couple of seconds to work out whether I'm Lucy or Alpha. But he's no longer scared of my sister. Ever since she risked her life trying to get him out of the shed, he's decided that while they are not quite friends, they are not enemies either.

'It's me. I know I look different. It's a school uniform, see. Gra and I spent ages ironing it, so you'd better not crease or tear it,' I say, putting my hand between his ears. I stroke the soft suedey bit there, and it makes me think of the soft patch behind my left ear, where the hair is growing back.

44

Incredible Alpha

I've had 134 hours of practice over 7 weeks, and I still don't feel ready. My footwork is good, my passes are on point, but I don't quite have the same reach with my left hand. I'll get there with time. Unfortunately, time is something I don't have.

'The outcome is much, much better than I could have expected,' said Dr Tinbar. 'With the damage done to the tendon between your thumb and forefinger, there was a high chance that you might have entirely lost the ability to grip. But your hand has healed well.'

'Does that mean I'll be able to carry on playing basketball?' I ask.

'Yes, when the bandages are off, I don't see why not. You'll need to go easy on yourself.'

'Keep playing, Alpha,' said Dad. 'I don't think you realise how good you are. Don't give up now.'

Every day I practised for a whole two hours after school with Josh. He's finished his exams and said he had nothing else to do, but I know Hector put in a good word.

I thought that I'd been giving it my all, but it wasn't until the incident with Claw that I'd really, properly started playing. Each time I was on the court was a reminder that I'd been given another chance – not only by the doctor, but also by the police.

I told PC Owusu what happened. She'd looked at me from behind her thick-rimmed glasses so seriously, I thought I was going to prison. Maybe it was because she'd seen what I'd put myself through to release Claw, or maybe it was because I'd owned up to everything, but I was eventually let off with a warning.

Vern and Hector got the same – although Vern protested until the very end that he hadn't been involved. Hector had to take out his phone to show the video footage of the night we took Claw to make him finally admit it.

Things have gone downhill significantly for Vern over the past few weeks. It turns out that he doesn't actually have a place at Bayville Academy, as he'd been claiming. His dad knew the Dean of Admissions there, and he must have thought that getting in was a done deal. But it wasn't so easy.

I could see how gutted he was about everything. He probably thought Hector and I would stop talking to him after what had happened with Claw. But I found that I couldn't stay angry with him for long. Mr Bray had been a bully, and I realised now that Mr Selling was too. I wanted to help Vern stand up to his dad.

I think he was surprised when I invited him and Hector to Whitecastle.

'It's really not as bad as I've been saying. Lucy and her friend Janus have some cool spots they can show us.'

He looked relieved as he nodded and quietly accepted my invitation.

As for me, I'm not about to give up on my dream.

'You really want to get a scholarship to Bayville?' Dad asked me, and I could see him trying to rack his brain over what he could do. I couldn't believe I'd ever thought he didn't care.

'We don't have the money right now, Alpha. But I did some research, and they're doing try-outs for their junior team. Anyone who does well has a good chance of getting into the academy in a couple of years' time. I reckon you should give it a go. This summer you're obviously not on top form, but maybe next year?'

'We'll be behind you all the way,' said Mum. She and I had made up properly. We both said sorry to each other at the same time – because we'd both said and done things that we didn't mean. Sometimes a dark storm cloud of anger can cover up the brilliant person you love – and it takes something unexpected to blow that cloud away.

Mum drove me to training with Josh almost every day. 'So that you'll be ready for next year,' she said.

I wouldn't be myself if I didn't do better than everyone expected. So here we are – Dad, Luce and me in the car, heading to the try-outs. I told Mum and Gra I didn't want a big crowd watching me, just the original Slam Dunk Trio.

'It'll take about an hour, Allie,' says Dad. 'Don't worry about the outcome. It's what you love doing. Enjoy it. Whatever happens – even if one day you're the NBA's biggest star – you'll never find better supporters than us.'

I know he's right.

When we get out of the car and walk into the Bayville Academy courtyard, he hugs me and whispers in my ear, 'You're already a star, Alpha. You always have been.'

And then Luce joins the hug too and I feel like my heart's about to explode, like the brightest supernova.

45

Two Hearts
Beating as One

I pan the telescope across to find Alpha Centauri, my sister's star, and then I do something I've only done once before with Dad. I don't know if I'll be able to find her on my own. I try to remember what he told me: 'First find Crux, and from its top point, move slightly north-west.'

She's probably too small to be seen through my telescope – last time we were using Dad's, which is bigger – but I end up finding her without any trouble. She's much brighter than I ever imagined, and she looks like she's pulsating from all the energy inside her.

Lucy.

I wonder if somewhere there's a star for a wolf named Claw.

Next to me, Alpha is asleep, but tomorrow I'll ask if she wants to look through my telescope. I'll show her Lucy and we'll do the dot-to-dot on the constellation of Gemini.

Maybe she'll ask if I remember that there's a bit of star right there in my palm, and in hers too.

'Yes,' I'll answer. 'A bit of supernova that blew up aeons ago. And now we're here to carry on its magic.'

Wolf rewilding

While *The Wolf Twins* is a fictional story, it's inspired by a real wolf rewilding programme in Yellowstone National Park, USA. In 1995, grey wolves were reintroduced to Yellowstone after being absent for nearly 70 years. This project was a huge success, with the wolf population recovering and bringing about ecological benefits such as helping elk to thrive and restoring plants that were under threat of extinction.

Wolf rewilding efforts are now underway in several European countries, including France, Germany, Sweden, Spain and Italy. These projects aim to restore wolf populations to their former ranges and promote the recovery of ecosystems.

Wolves are amazing creatures

Did you know...?

1. Wolves were once found in many parts of the world but faced threats from habitat loss and hunting. Efforts like rewilding have helped reintroduce them to certain areas, allowing them to thrive once again.
2. Wolves communicate through a variety of vocalisations, including howls, growls and barks. Howling helps them locate other pack members and communicate over long distances.
3. Wolves have a keen sense of smell, which helps them track prey and find their way. They also have excellent hearing, allowing them to detect even faint sounds.
4. Wolves are really important in nature because they are the top predators. They help keep things in balance by making sure there aren't too many prey animals, like deer, eating up all the plants.

A note on Whitecastle Forest

Whitecastle Forest is based on a real forest called Białowieża. Located on the border between Poland and Belarus, this ancient woodland is a true ecological gem. It spans over 1,500 square kilometers and is one of the largest remaining parts of primeval forest that once covered much of Europe.

Białowieża (literally translated as 'White tower' or 'White castle' forest) is renowned for its biodiversity. It is home to an incredible array of plant and animal species, including European bison, lynx and, of course, wolves. Some of its trees are exceptionally old, with lifespans reaching several centuries.

'Miejsce mocy' or 'The Place of Strength' which features in *The Wolf Twins* is also a real place in Białowieża. It's a small clearing among ancient trees, which, since medieval times, has been thought to have special healing powers. It's still visited every year by people seeking peace, reflection, and connection with nature.

Acknowledgements

The seed of this book first came about when I mentioned the Białowieża Forest to my agent, Kate Hordern. I was searching for the right story to set in this incredible primeval forest, which is home to so many wild creatures. Thank you Kate, for your great plot advice, unwavering support and encouragement.

A big thank you to my editors Lauren Atherton and Fiona Kennedy for your keen editorial eye and super insightful feedback – I really enjoy working with you! And to the wonderful team at Head of Zeus, particularly Meg, Jessie and Polly.

A special mention goes to Katy Riddell for her beautiful illustrations. I had a vision of what the cover should look like, but you exceeded this many times over! Thank you for bringing Alpha, Luce and Claw to life.

Thank you to all my family and friends, who continue to support my writing and often help me come up with amazing story details. And, of course, to Julia and Magda, my own twins, who are an endless source of inspiration.

A heartfelt thank you to all the booksellers, teachers, book bloggers, reviewers and fellow writers who have been so supportive of my books – with particular thanks to Kevin Cobane, Rich Simpson and Leanne Fridd (a fellow twin mum and owner of the fabulous *Bookbugs*).

Last but certainly not least, a big thanks to you, dear readers. I hope you enjoyed *The Wolf Twins*. Let's discover the supernovas inside us all!

Ewa Jozefkowicz

Zephyr is an imprint of Head of Zeus.
At Zephyr we are proud to publish books
you can read and re-read time and time
again because they tell a brilliant story
and because they entertain you.

@_ZephyrBooks

@_zephyrbooks

HeadofZeusBooks

readzephyr.com

www.headofzeus.com

ZEPHYR